Five Nights at Freddy's™

FAZBEAR FRIGHTS #8

GUMDROP ANGEL

Five Nights at Freddy's™

FAZBEAR FRIGHTS #8

GUMDROP ANGEL

BY

**SCOTT CAWTHON
ANDREA WAGGENER**

Scholastic Inc.

Library of Congress Cataloging-in-Publication Data available

ISBN 978-1-338-73998-5

1 2021

Printed in the U.S.A. 23

First printing 2021 • Book design by Jeff Shake

TABLE OF CONTENTS

Angel opened her eyes and saw . . . nothing. Darkness. Had she gone blind? She tried to blink but found she couldn't. Was she even worse off now than before?

She felt weak and heavy. Her body ached. Angel raised her hands to try and rub her eyes, to clear the guck from them, but her hands whacked against something hard.

Trying not to panic, she groped around to figure out what she'd hit. All she felt was wood, flat, smooth, unrelenting wood, surrounding her.

She was in some kind of box! A very small box.

Angel tried to scream, but her mouth wouldn't work properly. She began writhing her body, flailing her limbs. But it did no good. She just kept banging against the box.

She was trapped. And she felt really strange, woozy, like she was going to pass out.

Why was this happening to her?

Angel really wished she had earplugs. And nose plugs. And blinders.

No, skip all that.

Angel really wished for the ability to teleport. Yeah, that would be good. If she could teleport, she could just instantly go someplace else.

But first she'd have to be invisible so she could get away with teleporting. Or maybe she could have super-powers so she could just obliterate everything that was here.

No, that might be a little extreme. Teleporting would be good enough.

Where would she go? Pretty much anywhere but here—a landfill, a sewer, the most dangerous part of town. She could think of a million horrible places that would be an improvement on her current situation. After all, what could possibly be worse than here?

Angel and her family were in Freddy Fazbear's Pizza,

and if there was a place on earth that was more like hell than this, Angel didn't know about it. Freddy's was bad enough on its own: a relentlessly bright and cheery place with decor in strictly primary colors and a headache-inducing black-and-white checkerboard floor. But then you added the children. No, not just children. *Amped-up children*. Crazed, overexcited, peeing-in-the-ball-pit, puking-in-the-arcade children. Not much was worse than a few dozen little kids having a birthday party. It was obnoxious mixed with miserable topped with *Shoot. Me. Now.*

Angel looked around, and she had to admit that some of her distaste—all right, maybe all of it?—could have been related to envy and resentment. Her birthday had been the month before, and no one had thrown her a party of any kind.

Maybe at some point in Angel's life, she could have appreciated a kid's birthday party. Theoretically, she would have liked having her own birthday party here when she was little. She was sure if she'd had a party, she wouldn't have been as loud and insufferable about it as the kids in Freddy's were. She would have been happy, yes, but she would have been graceful about it . . . at least, she liked to think so. But then again, she'd never get to test that theory.

Seeing as her dad—not her current pathetic excuse for a stepdad, but her biological father (equally pathetic, apparently)—left when she wasn't even walking yet, her mother had to be both the moneymaker and the full-time parent. During those years, her mom had disappeared into her job, while somehow staying in a constant state of broke.

There was just never enough money for things like birthday parties. Now that Angel's mom had married Myron—aka "call me Dad," no, thank you very much—parties like this were in the budget, but, well . . . Angel was older and so over ostentatious displays of birthday frivolity.

And, come on, was a little kid's birthday honestly important enough to spend thousands of dollars on balloons, pizza, soda, cake, candy, and presents? No way. It was a waste of resources. That money could've bought Angel a car or paid tuition for the performing arts college she wanted to attend. Thankfully, Angel had qualified for a student loan, based on her mom's low income in this last year before she married Myron. But Angel shouldn't have had to get financial help, not when Myron could more than afford to pay her way. She never did call him "Dad," but that was because he hadn't earned it. Wasn't a "dad" supposed to pay for his kid's education?

Angel looked at the woman who had gotten her into this screwed-up situation: her mother—her weak, self-interested, gold-digging mother. If only her mother paid half as much attention to her daughter as she did to her own looks. Still reasonably young, Angel's mom had bouncy short blonde hair, bright blue eyes, and a face she spent thousands of dollars a year to keep pretty. Forget homework help or mother-daughter dates; Angel's mom was too busy spending half the day working out or updating her wardrobe at the mall.

Maybe Angel's mom would have been halfway decent if she'd had a good partner by her side. But then again, maybe not. Angel's mom wasn't exactly a paragon of patience or understanding. She also wasn't very good at cooking, cleaning, organizing, or planning. She didn't have a cool job like film editor or fashion designer or talent agent. From observing her friends' mothers, Angel thought these were the qualities that went into being a great mom. The qualities her mother had—an expert at improving her own looks, a whiz at makeup and clothes shopping, a world-class champion of flirting with men, a connoisseur of sleeping in, and a master of self-absorption to the point that she forgot anything not associated with her own happiness—did not make her good mom material.

Behind Angel, a little girl squealed, hitting decibels that should have been illegal. Angel put her fingers in her ears.

"Stop that," Angel's mother snapped. "You're eighteen, not eight."

Oh, right. And that was her mother's other notable quality: star of bowing to whatever man was paying the bills at the time. The truth was that Angel's mom didn't like loud, screaming children any more than Angel did, but right now, she was playing the role of Myron's wife. And Myron's wife was the mother of a five-year-old. This meant Angel's mom had to pretend she was happy to be at this party, and part of that pretense was to chastise Angel for dropping the act.

Angel rolled her eyes. Her mother was pathetic. So was Myron. And so was Ophelia, Myron's revolting daughter. The whole family was pathetic. Even Angel was pathetic because she had to be part of this family.

She needed to get out of it.

She'd come so close to surviving her childhood without facing the stepdad thing. The whole time she'd been growing up, her mother had been looking for "the right husband and father," the right husband and father being one who had lots and lots of money. Angel had lost count of the number of men who had come and gone over the years. There'd always been some guy. Some of them had kids. Some of them didn't. But when Angel had been dragged along on "family dates," she'd had the comfort of knowing it was temporary. She didn't have to go home with the guy or the kids. But then her mom had met Myron. And Ophelia came with Myron.

Who named a kid Ophelia? Ophelia was Hamlet's lover, a woman who'd gone crazy because Hamlet had seemingly gone crazy. Did that seem like the best inspiration for a baby's name?

Curious about Ophelia's name, Angel had looked up the meaning of it. Ophelia was a Greek name, she discovered, and it meant "help," as in, "*Help*, I was named after a tragic mental case." It had made her laugh when she'd read that. She could hear Ophelia's chirpy little kid voice saying it now.

Speaking of the annoying squeaky voice . . .

"Don't you want some pizza?" Ophelia asked Angel.

Before Angel could answer, Ophelia said, "I'll share mine." Then she pushed a slice of the foul-smelling excuse for pizza toward Angel's face.

Angel hated Freddy's pizza—the sauce had way too much basil, which gave it the offensive smell and made it, as far as Angel was concerned, inedible. Ophelia missed Angel's mouth, and smeared Angel's jaw with sauce. She could feel her hair sticking to it, too.

Angel slapped Ophelia's hand. "Get that away from me."

Ophelia's face crumpled. She jerked back, and the pizza slice flew out of her hands, landing facedown on Angel's chest, before sliding into her lap.

Angel jumped up, and the pizza fell to the floor. She looked at the red stain on her good jeans. "You little brat!" she yelled at Ophelia.

Ophelia's chin quivered. Tears spilled from her eyes. "I was just trying to share."

"Don't yell at your sister!" Angel's mother cut in.

"She's not my sister!" Angel shouted. She grabbed for some paper napkins and wiped at her face and hair.

As she did, she noticed several kids and adults at surrounding tables were staring at her. Great. She'd managed to make a spectacle of herself, even in a room full of manic kids. She felt her face redden, and she sat down.

"Angel," Myron growled, throwing her a scathing look, which he reserved exclusively for his stepdaughter these days.

He turned to Ophelia. "Come here, my princess."

Ophelia, crying hard now, crawled into Myron's lap. "She hit me, Daddy. I was just trying to share my pizza." Ophelia raised her arm for Myron's inspection. There was nothing on her arm except pizza sauce, but Myron looked at the poor offended arm and kissed it. Then he turned on Angel.

"I didn't hit her," Angel said before he could say

anything. "I shoved her hand away." That wasn't technically true, but Angel would get grounded for a year if she admitted to hitting Ophelia.

Myron opened his mouth, but he was cut off by one of the animatronic performers on the stage in front of their table. Being "the birthday girl," Ophelia had to have a prominent place in the audience for the Fazbear Extravaganza show. They were two feet from the stage. If Angel had wanted to, she could have reached out and swiped frosting off Ophelia's five-foot-tall layered cake. It was sitting onstage, to the side of where the animatronics were going to perform.

Angel had been dreading the big show because she knew it would be loud and chaotic—over-the-top. Now, however, she was grateful for it. It was drawing attention away from the family drama playing out at their table.

Ophelia immediately forgot the assault on her precious arm. She turned to Myron. "Up, Daddy, up!" He dutifully repositioned her on his lap so she could stand on his thighs. The full skirt of Ophelia's yellow frilly dress puffed up into Myron's face. He kept a grip on Ophelia with one hand and shoved aside the tulle with his other.

Ophelia stared up at the stage with bright eyes. She wiggled her hips and threw her arms around in an awkward dance of some kind.

Angel hated Ophelia. The kid was a nuisance, always dragging out a board game or begging to "play pretend" with Angel. She would jump into bed with Angel almost every night with a book and a whine of "Will you read to me?"

Sometimes, Angel did read to Ophelia, but she resented the time it took. Angel was busy; she didn't have time for a little sister.

And then there were the horses. Ophelia had a thing about horses. Her whole room was filled with them: plush horses, plastic horses, wood horses . . . posters, photos, and oil paintings of horses. She had a huge rocking horse in her room, and—though she was getting too big for it—she "rode" it every day. So did her dolls. That was Ophelia's world. Horses and dolls. It was, in fact, the theme of today's party, too. Angel was so sick of horses . . . of hearing about them, reading stories about them, being forced to join Ophelia in playing with them.

When Ophelia had demanded that her birthday party be at Freddy's, which was, sadly, her favorite restaurant, Angel had pointed out that a party at Freddy's wouldn't be a horse-themed party, which was also what Ophelia wanted. Freddy's didn't have horse characters. But Ophelia wasn't deterred. She wanted what she wanted.

Usually, Freddy's parties were Freddy themed. So Myron had to negotiate with Freddy's manager to bring in special themed napkins, plates, hats, and decorations. He also bought every kid in the place a horse toy. Angel had heard enough pretend neighing today to last a lifetime.

"I love my party, Daddy," Ophelia cried out. She grinned, revealing pizza sauce–stained teeth and looking for all the world like some kind of cannibal. It wasn't a pretty picture.

Not that any picture with Ophelia in it could be pretty.

No matter how you dressed her up, Ophelia was truly an ugly little girl. Poor kid. That was the only thing that made Angel feel an ounce of kindness toward her. No question Ophelia was a thorn in Angel's side, but the poor thing couldn't help how she looked. Just as Angel got her mom's looks, Ophelia got Myron's.

For reasons Angel couldn't fathom, her mom thought Myron was a catch—not just because of the money; she actually thought he was handsome. Angel thought Myron was a gorilla. Tall and trunk-shaped, Myron had dark brown hair . . . all over his body. He was the hairiest man Angel had ever seen. Now, of course, Ophelia didn't inherit that trait from her daddy, but she did get his prominent brow ridge, large nose, and small eyes. She also got his long arms. She looked like a chimpanzee, which was sad. Chimpanzees were cute, but kids who looked like chimpanzees weren't.

On the stage in front of Ophelia, Freddy's animatronics were getting ready to perform, and an announcer, a male Freddy's employee wearing a top hat and a bright red tuxedo, was chattering away with the crowd. The announcer was young and blond, round-faced, and perpetually smiling.

"Is everyone having a super-duper time?" the announcer asked.

"Yes!" all the kids shouted.

Ophelia screeched her "yes" even louder. The sound sent a stab of pain through Angel's temples.

"Is everyone ready to have even *more* fun?" Freddy himself called out.

"Yes!" the kids chorused.

"Fun, more fun!" Ophelia squealed. She wiggled so spastically in her dad's lap, he almost dropped her.

"Are we all ready to rock and roll?" Freddy shouted.

Everyone in the restaurant, except Angel, yelled, "Yes!" And then the restaurant was filled with cheers.

Angel noticed Myron was giving his stepdaughter the evil eye around Ophelia's billowing yellow skirt. Angel didn't care. The restaurant was now far too loud for Myron to chew out Angel. Ignoring her stepdad, Angel left her family at the table and went in search of a restroom so she could try and salvage her jeans.

The long rectangular tables in Freddy's were crammed together, and they were all full of hyper little kids and a smattering of weary-looking adults. Angel had to twist this way and that to work herself free of the unruly pack.

When she was almost through the melee, Angel collided with one of Freddy's employees. As she started to say, "Excuse me," he turned toward her. She only got her first word out because she was looking at one of the cutest guys she'd ever seen, and he'd robbed her of the ability to speak.

"Sorry," the cute guy said. "I should have been looking where I was going."

Angel opened her mouth, and nothing came out.

The cute employee grinned at her and started to say something else, but that's when the animatronics onstage started belting out a rock song with ear-shriveling vocals. The singers, combined with the band's heavy-on-the drums-and-electric-guitars style, made speaking impossible.

Angel began to move on, but the cute employee took her hand and led her out of the dining area. She thought that was a little presumptuous, but she didn't protest because the hand was warm and strong . . . and it was attached to the cute employee. Also, he was pulling her away from the noise and the spastic mayhem both on the stage and in the audience.

Aware of the pizza sauce still in her hair, Angel raised a hand to swipe at her face. She wished she had a mirror so she could clean herself up.

If not for the pizza sauce, Angel would have been pretty confident about her appearance. Although her mom hadn't done much for Angel, she had passed on her good genes. Angel had her mother's blonde hair (only Angel's was shoulder-length), blue eyes, pleasant features, and slender body. Even though she wasn't much for fashion and cosmetics like her mother was, Angel had her own style. She didn't wear a ton of makeup; she simply lined her eyes with kohl and kept her lips glossed. She was into retro thrift store clothes, and she was a whiz with scarves and jewelry and other accessories. She liked playing with them so much she usually kept an extra scarf or strand of beads in her purse so she could change her look when it suited her. Today, she'd done some cool loops with a seventies belt around her narrow waist, and under that, she wore a filmy sixties peasant top that clung to her just right. If Ophelia hadn't decided to spill sauce all over her, Angel would have been fit for a date right now.

The cute guy led Angel down the hallway outside the dining room. The hallway, lined with cartoony pictures of Freddy's animatronic characters, ran along the length of the dining area, connecting Freddy's entrance with the back of the restaurant, which presumably was where the kitchen and offices were. The pictures were framed in bright yellow, and all the characters wore happy, jaunty expressions.

A few doors opened up off the hallway, including those to the restrooms. Angel eyed the ladies' room door as they passed it. She wished she could go in and clean herself up.

They were headed, though, toward the front door of the restaurant. Angel wondered if the cute employee was going to try and get her to leave with him. But he just took her to the little waiting area filled with red plastic chairs, which was near the entrance.

When they reached the chairs, the cute employee motioned to them. "Have a seat. I'll be right back." He darted back down the hall they'd just come down.

Angel wondered, even as her butt hit the molded plastic, why she was so dutifully doing what the guy wanted. Had she inherited more from her mom than she thought she had? Was she turning into a male-pleasing automaton?

Angel couldn't explain why, but she waited in the chair for at least a minute. Then, concerned that she was abdicating her entire sense of an independent self, Angel started to stand. Why had she let the guy drag her out here in the first place?

The cute employee reappeared. He was carrying several paper towels and a spray bottle of what looked like water. He sat down on the seat next to hers.

Wow, he was cute! Just a little taller than Angel, the guy was broad-shouldered, narrow-hipped, and clearly fit. With dark hair and dark eyes and strong features, he had the kind of looks that pretty much any girl with eyes would find attractive.

"I'm Dominic," the cute guy said. He had a wonderful voice, deep and resonant.

Angel involuntarily lowered herself back into the chair. "Angel," she said.

"Yes, you are."

Angel rolled her eyes.

Dominic grinned. "You've heard that one before. Of course you have."

Angel smiled. She couldn't help it. He was irresistible. "But you made it sound better than anyone else has."

Dominic laughed. "Now, *there's* a good line. I should take lessons from you."

Angel laughed. "No, that's a terrible idea. I just sort of blurt out whatever I'm thinking. That's not always the best thing."

"I disagree. Honesty is highly underrated."

A group of giggling little girls burst out of the dining room, ran down the hallway, and poured into the ladies' room like a swarm of frilly pink-clad bees. Angel was glad now she wasn't in the ladies' room.

She turned back to Dominic and figured she might as

well see where this encounter went. "Thank you for saving me."

"Did I? I was just doing my job. I'm an assistant manager here, and one of my duties is to make sure the customers are happy. I saw a pretty girl smeared with pizza sauce, and I figured she'd be happier if it was cleaned up." He raised the spray bottle and the paper towels.

Dominic reached out and touched Angel's pizza-sauce-crusted hair. "Not that you don't totally rock this Italian-food-in-the-hair look."

Angel laughed.

Dominic leaned toward her.

Angel held her breath.

"Do you mind?" Dominic said. "I don't think pizza sauce is a good conditioner, and as a hair color, well, this particular shade of red doesn't match the rest of your hair."

Angel said nothing. She was trying to remember what she last ate. She hadn't eaten any of the pizza her mom and Myron ordered. But she did have some chocolate candy. Well, that shouldn't have given her bad breath.

Dominic was dabbing at her hair and the skin of her jaw and neck with paper towels he'd sprayed with whatever was in the plastic bottle. Whatever it was smelled flowery, and it was warm. It felt soothing against the skin of her jaw and her ear, and he was being so gentle.

Who was this guy? It seemed like he came from an entirely different planet than the guys at her school. They were oafs by comparison. None of the guys she knew at her school would know how to clean pizza sauce out of hair.

"Okay. That's better," Dominic said. He tucked a strand of hair behind her ear. Then he looked down at her jeans. He held out more wet towels. "Think you can handle the rest? I don't want to be disrespectful."

Angel laughed and took the towels. "I appreciate that." She worked at the stain on her jeans. The deep red faded a little but didn't disappear. She hoped it would come out in the wash.

"So, I assume you're here with your family?" Dominic said, once Angel was cleaned up.

"Yeah. Sort of. My stepsister is the birthday girl."

"Ah. So, I *did* save you. Does she make you clean the fireplace and scrub the floor, too, Cinderella?"

"She would if she was old enough to care about that stuff. For now, her daddy, my stepdad, is the one on my case."

"Ah. Yeah, that can suck."

"Yes, it can."

"I haven't seen you before. What school do you go to?"

"I'm graduating from Merrimount in a month. You?"

"Same . . . graduating in a month. But from Graves Academy."

"Ooh. Snazzy." Graves Academy was a private school for brainiacs. Angel was impressed in spite of herself.

"Yeah, right?" Dominic gestured at his Freddy's vest and name tag. "I know I make this Freddy's thing look good, but you should see me in my school uniform. It would knock your socks off."

Angel looked down at her sandal-clad feet. So did Dominic.

"See?" Dominic said. "Even thinking about me in my uniform knocked your socks off."

Angel laughed even as she groaned.

Dominic smiled. "So, how did you end up wearing our pizza instead of eating it? Please tell me a server didn't get this sloppy."

"No. Not a server. Ophelia."

Dominic raised an eyebrow. "Hamlet's hapless lover?"

"Yeah, right. See? I was just thinking about that. Why would you name a child Ophelia?"

"I guess it's a pretty name, but it has some heavy connotations. And Ophelia is . . . ?"

"My stepsister."

"Ah, the wicked stepsister. 'Out, out damned spot.'"

Angel laughed. "I think you're suffering from Shakespearean confusion."

"'Something wicked this way comes,'" Dominic said.

Angel laughed harder. "Better sentiment, but you're still in the wrong play."

"Ah well. 'This above all, to thine own self be true.'"

"Ding. Ding. Ding. Give the man a prize," Angel said. "He made his way back to *Hamlet*."

They both laughed, and then they both spoke at once. Angel said, "Thank you for . . ." just as Dominic said, "Listen, how about . . . ?"

They both stopped and grinned.

Before either could finish a sentence, a woman's voice called out, "Dominic."

Angel and Dominic turned toward the voice.

Another Freddy's employee, a thirtysomething woman, stood just outside the dining room. "There you are," she said.

The woman was tall and athletic-looking, with brown hair caught up in a ponytail. She wore a Freddy's uniform, and she looked perfectly calm in spite of the chaos swirling around her.

Dominic stood. "Hey, Nancy. I'm coming."

"Meet me in the kitchen," Nancy said.

Dominic turned and held out his hand. Angel took it. She was happy to have the chance to hold his hand again.

"I'm sorry to abandon you to all this"—he waved his arms out—"and your evil stepsister, too, but duty calls."

"No problem."

He smiled at her. "Before my boss so rudely interrupted, I was about to ask if you might like to go out tomorrow night. There's an indie band playing at the Rocket House. Would you be game?"

"Sure, I'd like that."

"Great. If you give me your number, I can pick you up. If you don't want to give me your number, you could meet me there."

Angel rattled off her home phone number.

Dominic laughed. "Okay, then." He repeated the number back to her, and she nodded.

"You won't forget it?" she asked when he didn't write it down. She wanted to kick herself because she sounded like a nag.

He didn't seem to mind. "I have a great memory. I won't forget it. Or you."

Angel blushed.

Dominic reached into the pocket of his uniform vest. "And here. Here's my Freddy's card. You can always call me."

Angel took the card and stuck it in her jeans pocket.

"But you won't have to call me," Dominic said. "I'll beat you to it. I'm going to be working here late tonight. Lots of cleanup to do and then prep for another party tomorrow. I'll call you later this evening to set up the time," Dominic said.

Angel nodded.

"Are you heading back in?" Dominic asked her.

She shrugged, then nodded. "I guess I have to."

Dominic laughed and offered his arm. "Then may I escort you to the pandemonium, milady?"

Angel laughed and took his arm. "You may, Prince Charming."

Dominic chuckled and led her back into the dining room. He squeezed her hand briefly before letting her go in the doorway. "Until later," he said.

She nodded.

"Where have you been?" Myron demanded when Angel got back to her family's table.

The band was getting ready for a sing-along.

Angel glared at him. "I had to go clean up the pizza sauce your klutzy daughter decided to smear all over me."

Angel's mom leaned in. "The snarky attitude isn't necessary. Ophelia is only five years old, Angel."

"Yeah, I know. And yet, she's the head of the household. How does that make sense?"

Myron shook his head.

The sing-along started, and Angel noticed Dominic, who was now singing, too, moving gracefully from table to table. His voice could be heard above the din of all the kids' voices. He had a really nice voice!

As she watched him singing with a trio of rambunctious boys, Angel wondered if Dominic wanted to be a performer. That was what she was going to be. Angel was going to be an actress, singer, and dancer. She was equally talented at all three. Truly. All the teachers in the drama and music department at her high school had told her she was talented enough to make it in the entertainment industry. They were the ones who'd encouraged her to apply to the performing arts school. She probably wouldn't have had the confidence to do it without their urging.

"Audiences are just going to eat you up, Angel," her favorite drama teacher had said when she'd given Angel the application. "You're going to be special, unlike any other."

When she'd applied to school, Angel had no idea how she was going to pay for it because Myron said he wasn't paying for "some art school that can't prepare you for the real world." She was thrilled that she qualified for loans.

Angel watched Dominic dance a sort of modified rumba with a few little kids. Their faces shined with joy. It was strange—earlier today this same scene would've had Angel rolling her eyes, but watching how good Dominic was with the kids . . . it made her see this place in a whole different light.

Her mother poked Angel's arm. "Why aren't you singing? You love to sing."

Angel shrugged. Her mom had a point. Why not sing? So she sang.

"Not so loud," her mother said immediately.

Angel stopped singing and crossed her arms. She tried to return to Dominic watching, but a group of kids were now dancing on chairs, and they blocked her line of sight.

Another eternity later, the singing stopped and finally the announcer made a big production of bringing Ophelia up on the stage to blow out candles on the gargantuan cake. Of course, Ophelia couldn't even manage her five candles. The animatronics helped her. Angel vaguely wondered how that worked. They must have had little blowers in their mouths.

After Ophelia received claps, whistles, and a standing ovation for blowing out two of her five candles, servers began cutting and passing out cake while the animatronics continued performing. Angel slouched in her chair watching the animatronics dance. She wished she could re-choreograph their routine.

As soon as the cake had been doled out, microphone feedback pierced through the commotion, and the announcer called out, "And now for the grand finale of today's festivities. May we have the birthday girl back onstage, please?"

Ophelia grinned and ran up to the stage. Everyone cheered again.

Angel looked around the room until she spotted Dominic. He was talking to his boss at the edge of the dining room, but he saw her glancing his way. He winked at her.

Angel smiled. Maybe things were looking up. It was, after all, only a month to graduation, and then she was going to stay with a friend in another state while they attended a summer-long acting workshop. Angel got a scholarship for it, and she'd been saving up for travel and food expenses, which was all she needed since her friend wasn't going to charge her rent. Then after that, performing arts school! Pretty soon, she'd be living her own life, making her own choices, and she wouldn't have to take any more orders from Myron or play second fiddle to Ophelia.

"And now for the pièce de résistance," the announcer shouted. "Lower away!"

The band played a loud fanfare, and something started coming down from the ceiling. Angel figured they were about to see a Freddy-shaped piñata or something. Piñatas seemed to be popular at kids' birthday parties these days.

Only half watching the thing get lowered down, Angel blinked and looked more carefully when she saw that the object wasn't a piñata. At least, it wasn't a piñata that looked like any she'd seen before.

Sinking slowly down into the room, a sort of soft-looking statue was undulating and quivering its way closer and closer to the stage. The statue was vaguely girl-shaped, and it wasn't made of papier-mâché.

It seemed to be made of . . . was that candy?

Angel leaned forward and squinted. Yeah. It looked like gummy candy. It was like a big gummy statue. Okay. That was different.

Interested now, even as she was equally repelled, Angel watched the gummy statue throw out its arms, kick its legs, and gyrate its body. Clearly some form of animatronic like Freddy and his band members, the gummy statue was in constant motion. It flung itself this way and that.

Weird. Gross. And maybe a little cool.

"Kids," the announcer called out, "for your eating enjoyment, we present to you the Birthday Gummy!"

The kids cheered.

The announcer looked at Ophelia. "You, my lovely young lady, as the birthday girl, have the privilege of taking the first bite of our yummy gummy. You will start with the yummy gummy's toes. And you get the responsibility of having the last bite, the yummy gummy's gumdrop nose."

Ophelia laughed and clapped her hands. She started toward the gummy statue.

The announcer held up a hand. "Before you start, dear birthday girl, let me repeat to you all. Only the birthday girl can take the gumdrop nose. That is for Ophelia and only for Ophelia. Does everyone understand?"

The kids all chorused, "Yes!"

"Excellent," the announcer said.

"Now you may begin, Ophelia, and then, kids, come on up and join her. You will all need to take bites to devour this yummy gummy! Ready, set, go!"

Ophelia ran over to the gummy statue and bit off its big toe. Even though it was made of candy, watching Ophelia eat the toe made Angel feel a little sick. She thought it was strange that the gummy statue kept moving even as the other kids filled the stage and began chewing their way up the statue's legs. Angel would have thought they would have turned off the animatronics before the thing got eaten.

Bored again now that the gummy was being consumed by scrabbling children, Angel sat back and tapped her foot. For a few minutes, she watched the kids eat the candy, but then she started feeling queasy. The scene reminded her of the horrible nature shows Myron liked to watch, the ones where the lions ran down a zebra and chowed down. Angel hated those shows.

"It's just nature, Angel," Myron would say to her when she objected. "Quit being so squeamish."

Nature or not, she didn't like seeing living things eaten. She didn't even like seeing the lobsters in the tanks at restaurants.

The gummy statue was just a little *too* lifelike to enjoy seeing it devoured by a hoard of little kid mouths. So by the time the kids were halfway up the legs, she had reached into her purse and come up with a nail file. She started touching up her nails.

Another several years passed, and the announcer shouted, "You're doing great, kids! Remember, the gumdrop nose is for Ophelia, and only Ophelia."

Angel glanced up to see the kids were at the neck. Only the statue's head was left. It had been lowered closer to the stage so the kids could reach it. Angel watched a pudgy kid tear off the head's ear with his little white teeth. Her stomach flip-flopped. She looked back down at her nails.

She didn't look up again until the announcer shouted, "Everyone, stop!"

The kids froze.

The head was almost gone.

"Ophelia, our birthday girl, come get your gumdrop nose," the announcer called.

Angel looked up once more. She saw Ophelia sitting at the edge of the stage looking like she might be sick. The announcer, unperturbed, danced over, pulled her to her feet, and escorted her to the remains of the gummy statue.

"Take your gumdrop nose," the announcer said.

Ophelia looked at the announcer, then reached out and plucked the nose from the nearly consumed head. She tugged on the announcer's leg, and he bent over. She whispered something to him, and he stood, "Our birthday girl is going to take her gumdrop nose home to savor at a later time. Let's give her a big round of applause."

For what, Angel wondered, *saving a gumdrop for later? Please.*

Angel shook her head and waited for the century that had been Ophelia's birthday party to come to an end.

They finally left Freddy's at around 6:00 p.m. Considering they'd left the house before noon, Angel decided it had to have been one of the longest birthday parties on record.

The sun was still in the sky, reminding Angel how close they were to June and graduation, her ticket to freedom. The thought helped loosen some of her taut muscles.

Angel got into the back seat of Myron's "top-of-the-line" minivan and strapped herself in while Myron helped Ophelia into her car seat. Ophelia said she was feeling "bloopy" because she ate too much of the gummy statue. She still hadn't eaten the gumdrop nose, though; it had been wrapped carefully in plastic for her.

Ophelia stank of sweat and garlic. Angel shrunk against her door and turned to look out the window. She pressed her nose against the warm glass and tried to breathe the sun's expansive rays through the glass instead of Ophelia's stench.

Myron finished strapping in his precious daughter and then got in the driver's seat. Angel's mom was already in the passenger seat, visor down, checking her makeup.

Myron started the engine and then turned around to look at Ophelia. "So are you ready for your big birthday surprise, sweetie?"

Angel swiveled to gawk at Myron. He had to be kidding. There was more than that extravagant birthday display they'd just endured?

Ophelia, who had been about to nod off before Myron spoke, lifted her head and clapped her hands. "Birthday surprise?! What is it, Daddy?"

"You'll have to wait and see, my princess."

Ophelia bounced in her car seat. She grinned at Angel and asked, "Do you know what my surprise is?"

Angel shook her head and turned toward the window again. She did her best to zone out as the minivan began moving, and she must have done a good job because the next thing she knew, Myron was shouting, "Here we are!"

Ophelia let out an adult-size snort and opened her eyes. Angel blinked and wiped her wet eyes. Then she blinked again and wiped her eyes again.

No.

Really?

Myron had pulled the minivan into a graveled area in front of a huge barn, next to a grassy paddock in which three lovely chestnut horses grazed. The evening sun caressed their backs, turning them golden.

"Horsies!" Ophelia squealed. "Oh, Daddy, are there ponies? I want a pony!"

"I know, sweetie," Myron laughed. He got out of the minivan and opened the back door to unstrap his daughter.

"Come on, Angel," her mother said.

Angel forced herself to open the minivan door. She had to command her feet to move. She did not want to see what was about to happen.

She got out of the car and looked around. Myron, Ophelia, and Angel's mom were heading toward the barn, and they didn't seem to care she wasn't with them. So, Angel turned in the opposite direction. She picked her way across the gravel, listening to her footsteps crunch, and she approached the wood fence around the paddock. One of the horses, a mare, trotted over to see her, dropping her huge head over the top of the fence to nuzzle Angel's shoulder.

The mare smelled like fresh hay and moist earth. She also smelled a little like manure. Or maybe that wasn't the horse. The paddock needed cleaning up.

Angel laughed when the mare gave Angel an insistent shove with her nose. "I don't have anything for you," she said.

"Do you want to give her an apple?"

Angel turned to see a redheaded girl coming her way. The girl's long hair was plaited into a braid, and she was smiling. She wore denim overalls, and she looked open and friendly.

"Hi," Angel said.

"Hi." The girl held out a slice of apple.

Angel took it.

"Put it in your palm and hold your palm out flat and steady," the girl said.

Angel did as she was instructed.

The horse took the apple slice. Her lips felt warm and soft against Angel's palm. The puff of her breath tickled.

Angel smiled. "You're awesome," she told the horse.

"Thanks," the redheaded girl said.

Angel looked at her.

"Oh, you weren't talking to me?" The girl laughed. "I get that all the time. Next to the horses, I tend to disappear."

"Sorry," Angel said. "My name's Angel."

"Tammy."

"You work here?" Angel asked.

Tammy nodded. "This is my dad's place."

"That's my mom and stepdad over there," Angel said. "Ophelia is getting a pony."

"Ophelia?"

Angel pointed. "My stepsister."

"Oh yeah. Sweet little girl. She's been out here a couple times to ride the ponies. But today she's hitting the jackpot."

Angel ignored the "sweet little girl" comment. "What do you mean by 'the jackpot'?"

"Oh, I mean Ophelia isn't just getting a pony. She's getting a pony *and* a horse. Her dad wants her to have the pony while she's still small, but he's bought a yearling for her, too. He wants her to grow up with her horse, and she's going to be getting private lessons all year long, too."

"How much does that cost?" Angel blurted. "Sorry. That was rude, and you probably can't tell me."

"No, I get it. And I don't think there's any confidentiality in our business, at least not this part of it. Now, if we were talking racehorses, that would be another corral of fillies."

Angel smiled.

"The pony's two thousand dollars," Tammy said. "The yearling is three thousand dollars. But that's just the beginning. We charge a couple thousand a year to keep and take care of a pony or a horse, so your stepdad will be spending about four thousand dollars a year on fees and then the lessons will be fifty dollars a day. So, let's say she comes an average of three times a week even, for fifty weeks, that's . . . what?" Tammy looked upward, doing math in her head.

"That's seven thousand five hundred a year," Angel said.

"Yeah," Tammy said. "So, what did *you* get for your birthday this year?"

Angel laughed. "Dinner at a burger place . . . because that was where Ophelia wanted to go. I'm a vegetarian."

"Oh, that's rude."

"I know, right? But I also got a small cake, and a new set of suitcases, you know, for when I leave home."

Tammy barked out a laugh. "Oh, sorry. That's so sad it's funny." Tammy covered her mouth. "I'm so sorry."

Angel laughed, too. "It's all right. They say comedy is tragedy plus time."

Tammy shook her head. "I was feeling sorry for myself before I came over here to talk to you. See, I want to go to culinary school, and my dad won't let me go until the fall because his foreman got injured and I need to stay and help. I mean, once Ed, the foreman, is back, Dad will pay for my school, and he's even getting me a car."

Angel sighed.

"I'm not bragging," Tammy said. "I'm only telling you so I can hear how good I actually have it. I really am sorry you're stuck with a jackass of a stepdad. Really sorry."

Angel shrugged. "Well, I'm glad I can hang here and make *you* happy."

It was well after 8:30 p.m. when they finally got home. Ophelia was asleep again when Myron pulled the minivan into the garage. Angel was numb.

She was only breathing, she thought, because it was

habit. She was in shock, so angry that she had no clue how to process it. She just couldn't believe what had happened. No, that wasn't true. She *did* believe it. And that's what made her so angry.

"So did you love your party and your surprise, my princess?" Myron asked Ophelia as they came through the mudroom and laundry room from the four-car garage.

Angel ignored Myron and his daughter as she cut through the kitchen and headed up the stairs to her bedroom. Her mom, and then Myron and Ophelia, followed her. She listened to the echo of their footfalls as they traipsed over the expensive hardwood floors that Myron was inordinately proud of. The house sounded so cavernous, so cold and uninviting. It was big, but who cared?

Myron and Angel's mother had the biggest bedroom in the house, naturally. It was a huge master suite with a sitting area. Ophelia's room, though, wasn't much smaller. Her domain was also a suite, with a sleeping area, a reading nook, and a play area. She also had her own huge closet and bathroom.

Angel got a normal-size room at the end of the hall, and she didn't get her own bathroom. She had to walk to the other end of the hall to use a bathroom. *Whatever.* She'd be gone soon enough.

Angel went into her plain peach-and-white room. Myron had had it decorated, without Angel's input. She hated the colors. She hated the sheer curtains, and she hated the twin-size bed. She was almost an adult. She deserved at least a full-size bed. The only thing Angel liked about her room was the view. Her window looked out over the back-yard, which was huge and filled with trees.

Flopping down on her tiny bed, Angel clenched her teeth and thought about the unfairness of it all. What was she? Trash? Something to be ignored and discarded?

Angel stood and started pacing back and forth. One day, one day very soon, Myron, her mother, and Ophelia, too, would realize how wrong they were to dismiss her. Angel was not going to be ignored. She was going to be success-ful, hugely successful, and when she was, she wasn't going to share a dime with her horrible mother and stepdad and stepsister. She was going to make it. She was going to be the center of attention.

Angel dropped onto her bed again. She thought about just going to sleep. The day had totally drained her. But her stomach wouldn't stop growling. So, she left her room and headed for the kitchen.

As she went back down the hall, Angel glanced, more from habit than from interest, into Ophelia's room. Ophelia was nowhere in sight. She was probably in the master with her daddy. Angel saw the plastic-wrapped gumdrop nose sitting on Ophelia's white-painted nightstand. She noticed Ophelia had placed the nose in her "treasures" dish, a little crystal (yes, real crystal) shallow bowl that held everything from rocks and seashells to coins and gold jewelry. Angel shook her head and continued on.

Back downstairs, Angel went into the kitchen and flipped on the light switch. Warm yellow glowing circles shined down from the amber glass pendants above the tanker-size island and illuminated black granite counter-tops. Recessed lights lit up custom cherry cabinets, and stainless-steel appliances. The kitchen was a gourmet cook's dream. Too bad a gourmet cook didn't live here.

Angel cooked a little but not a ton. She'd had to learn what little she knew how to cook on her own. Come to think of it, she'd had to learn *everything* she knew how to do on her own.

She went to the fridge, scrounged around, and found a bean salad she'd made for herself a couple days before. She was about to take the first bite when the phone rang.

Thinking of Dominic, she snatched up the receiver. "Hello?"

"Ah, I think I hear the voice of an Angel," Dominic said.

"Very funny." Angel thought she sounded casual and relaxed, but her pulse had at least doubled its pace the second Dominic spoke.

"I *am v*ery funny, aren't I? Aren't you lucky to have met me?"

Angel laughed. "I'm beside myself."

"There are two of you? Lucky me."

Angel groaned but giggled. "You do think you're funny, don't you?"

"Hilarious."

Angel shook her head. "And also very modest."

"Very."

"Not to mention succinct," Angel said, smiling.

Dominic chuckled. "'Brevity is the soul of wit.'"

"Good one," Angel said. "Proud of yourself?"

"Inordinately."

Angel laughed. She had to admit she was impressed that he'd thrown out another *Hamlet* quote. But she wasn't going to tell him that. "You're too much."

"'The lady doth protest too much, methinks,'" Dominic said.

Angel groaned.

A click came over the line, and Myron's heavy breathing battered Angel's ear. "I'm on the phone, Myron," she said.

"It's late. Who are you talking to?"

Late? It isn't even 9:00 p.m.!

Angel was going to lie and say it was one of her friends, but Dominic, clueless about the extent of Myron's unreasonableness, spoke up. "My name is Dominic, sir. I'm calling to ask out your stepdaughter."

"Who the hell are you?" Myron asked. "I've never heard her talk about a Dominic."

"I just—" Angel tried to insert.

"We just met today, sir," Dominic said innocently.

Angel groaned.

"Where? Are you lying? She was with us. Where do you get off lying to me, young man?"

Dominic spoke . . . after a slight hesitation. He seemed to be getting that Myron wasn't playing with a full deck. "I know she was with you today, sir," Dominic said in the slow soothing tone one used to pacify a distressed toddler. "She was at Freddy's with your family. I work part-time there. I'm one of the assistant managers."

"I didn't see you," Myron snapped.

Another little silence preceded Dominic's patient response. "With all due respect, sir, you wouldn't know if you did see me. We haven't met yet."

"That's exactly my point. You're not taking Angel out. We don't know you."

"I'm happy to come over and—" Dominic began.

"You're not coming to this house. We don't know you," Myron repeated.

"I'm sorry, but how will you get to know me if you don't meet me?"

"Get the hell off my phone, smart aleck," Myron said. He slammed down his receiver and bellowed down the stairs. "You'd better be off in ten seconds, Angel, or I'm coming down there."

Angel cringed. "I have to go," she said to Dominic.

"Call me when you can," Dominic said. Angel hung up the phone just as Myron stomped into the kitchen.

"Where do you get off handing out my phone number to a total stranger?" he demanded.

"It's *my* phone number, too," Angel pointed out.

"Just by happenstance," Myron said.

"What's that supposed to mean?"

"It means I married your mother, and you came along for the ride."

"I *came along for the ride*?!" Angel threw back, incredulous. She widened her eyes and stared at Myron.

Her mom came into the room. She held up a small stack of envelopes. "I got the mail. Angel, you got a letter."

Angel took the letter her mother held out, and she

glanced at the return address. It was from the student loan office. Maybe they were going to give her more money. She ripped the envelope open and looked at the letter.

She read a couple sentences. "What?" she blurted.

"What is it?" her mother said.

Angel looked up at her mother. "They're rescinding my student loan offer because they updated their records and discovered you're now married to Myron, and Myron makes too much money for me to qualify for a loan."

"Well, he does make a lot of money," her mother said.

"But how does that help me?" Angel shouted. She whirled to face Myron. "Are you going to pay for me to go to school?"

"Not that stupid art school."

"But that's the school I want to go to. It's a good school, a nationally ranked school."

"I don't care. It's not a normal college. I'm not paying for something that isn't a normal college. Shouldn't have to pay for anything at all, come to that, but as a gift to my beloved Bianca, I'd pay for you to go to a state college. That's the deal. Take it or leave it."

"But you can afford it," Angel argued. "You wouldn't even notice the money missing. The amount of money I need to go to school is nothing to you."

"You have a lot to learn about money, young lady," Myron said.

Angel couldn't keep it inside anymore. She hadn't said a word at the horse farm. She hadn't made a peep in the car. But it came out now.

"You just bought your daughter two horses!" Angel screamed. "She's five! You're going to spend more on those horses and on her horseback riding lessons in the next few years than you would on all of my education plus a car. How is horseback riding better than a performing arts school? At least I'm going to school to learn a skill I can use to make a living. What good will riding horses do for Ophelia? She's going to be way too big to be a jockey."

"Don't you insult your sister!" Myron shouted.

"She's not my sister!" Angel yelled for the second time today. "She's *your daughter*, and she's a thief."

"What the hell does that mean?" Myron demanded.

"She stole what should have been mine. She stole my mother, and she's stealing my future. It isn't fair."

"Life *isn't* fair," Myron said, smirking.

"You're ruining my life!" Angel yelled.

She turned to her mother. "If you hadn't married this ass, we'd be poor, yeah, but at least we'd both be happy. At least I'd be able to get a student loan!"

"I'm very happy," her mother said woodenly.

"Yeah, and I'm a piñata," Angel said. She picked up the open plastic container of bean salad, and she threw it in the sink. The container bounced up on impact, and beans flew everywhere.

Angel ran out of the kitchen.

"You get back here and clean that up," Myron yelled.

"Clean it up yourself," Angel yelled back. "It's your freaking house!"

Angel took the stairs two at a time. She reached the hall

and stomped down it, intending to go into her room, throw herself on the bed, and cry her eyes out. But as she passed Ophelia's room, her peripheral gaze landed on the plastic wrapper with the gumdrop nose.

Angel stopped. She looked at the nose. And she saw Ophelia, wearing a new pair of horse-motif pajamas, sitting in her play area happily talking to her baby dolls, which were riding on plush horses.

Angel couldn't help herself. If she was going to have a treasure taken from her, the treasure of going after her dream, of being able to live her life the way she wanted to live it, Ophelia had to lose a treasure, too. Fair was fair.

Angel charged into Ophelia's room.

"Wanna play horsey rides?" Ophelia asked.

Angel ignored her. She strode to Ophelia's nightstand and snatched up the wrapped gumdrop nose.

"Hey," Ophelia said. "That's mine!"

Ophelia started to scramble to her feet, but she tripped over her big plush horse-head slippers. She landed on her hands and knees and started crying.

"Yeah? Well, it's mine now." Angel unwrapped the nose and popped it into her mouth.

"No!" Ophelia screamed. She thrashed out of her slippers, stood, and ran toward Angel. "Stop!" she yelled.

It was too late.

"Mm, good," Angel said, chewing dramatically.

Actually, it wasn't good at all. It tasted horrible. Like sugar and . . . she didn't know what. It was just a sugary yuck. But she chewed and swallowed it anyway.

Ophelia squawked like a bird and then began howling like a deranged wolf. Angel could hear her mother and Myron thundering up the stairs. She shot an imaginary gun at Ophelia, and said, "Catch you later, kid."

Then she darted to her room just as Myron got to the top of the stairs. Ophelia continued to howl, and Angel didn't care at all.

She went into her room and shut and locked the door. For good measure, because she could hear Myron's raised voice and heavy steps in the hall, she put her desk chair under the knob.

She worked her tongue around inside her mouth trying to get rid of the disgusting taste of the gumdrop nose. But even as she did, she felt a nauseating sense of self-satisfaction. It felt distressingly good to make Ophelia feel bad. For once, Angel was able to take something from Ophelia instead of the other way around.

It made her feel small and ashamed that she was so triumphant.

See? There. Ophelia had just stolen something else: Angel's self-respect.

Myron pounded on her door and shouted something unintelligible. She tensed.

Myron had never hit her or anything . . . he'd only used his words to berate her. But she didn't know what Myron would do to her for eating Ophelia's precious nose. She giggled. That sounded funny.

The roaring outside her door wasn't funny, though. She stopped giggling. She backed up and sat on her bed.

Not for the first time, she wished she had a phone in her room. She wanted to call Dominic. Or her friends. Or the police. Someone had to be on her side.

"Get out here, young lady," Myron yelled outside her door. "You've gone too far this time!"

She didn't respond to him. She just sat on her bed, hugged her knees to her chest, and rocked herself.

When Myron kept shouting and pounding on her door, she turned off her lights and put on her headphones. She closed her eyes and began singing along with her favorite song. Singing would make her feel better.

Angel woke up abruptly. Where was she?

She rubbed her eyes and tried to orient herself. The last she remembered, she was listening to music and singing. She looked around the room. It was dark.

She flipped on the lamp on her nightstand and looked at her clock. It was just past 11:00 p.m. She took off her headphones and listened. The house was silent except for the intermittent ticks and groans—the usual sounds.

Angel's neck itched. She scratched at it. Her jaw itched, and she scratched at that as well. When the itching started up on her chest, she got up and went to her dresser so she could look in the mirror. Had she gotten bitten by some insect at the horse farm?

Angel looked at her reflection. She sucked in her breath.

Even in the soft light from her nightstand, Angel could see the skin of her jaw, neck, and upper chest were mottled bright red and unnaturally pale white; the skin was all puffy and angry-looking. It looked like a rash, but not like a rash she'd ever seen before.

Angel touched her inflamed skin. It felt weird, like it had a squishy texture.

She stared at herself in horror. Oh, this was so not good. Not good at all.

Angel didn't like to think of herself as super wrapped up in how she looked, because that was something she hated about her mother, but she had to admit, she tended to take her looks for granted. She was pretty, and she knew it. She didn't use her looks to gain an unfair advantage or anything. She didn't let her looks turn her into an idiot, either. Boys at school asked her out all the time, but she usually said no. She'd only dated a couple guys, and she'd found them to be immature and grabby. She'd never let anything pro-gress pass a few dates. She'd never had a boyfriend, either. Dominic was the first boy she'd considered to be boy-friend material.

But Angel's looks were an integral part of her plan to be a successful actress, singer, and dancer. She was going into an industry that valued looks almost even above talent. Getting some kind of weird skin condition a month before an acting workshop was the exact opposite of what she needed.

She stared at the blotchy mass of bright red nodules on her skin, and as she watched, the redness spread. It was spreading fast. She could actually see it creeping up from her jawline to the lower part of her cheek.

Maybe it was some sort of rash from the horses at the

stable? She had been feeling a little congested at the barn. Ophelia and her horrible father had taken everything from her—it only made sense that they'd be responsible for taking her health, too.

"Oh, stop, please stop," Angel pleaded as she watched the ugliness fan outward from her jaw and creep up her lovely smooth cheeks.

What could she do?

Angel went to her door, listened, heard nothing, and carefully opened the door. As soon as the door was open, she could hear Myron's reverberant snores coming through the double doors to the master suite. The louder blasts nearly vibrated the whole house. How did her mother sleep next to that man?

With earplugs, that was how. Her mom bought the best earplugs money could buy.

Ophelia was snoring, too. Her snores were like mini versions of her dad's.

Angel tiptoed down the hall, went into the bathroom, shut the door as quietly as she could, and then turned on the bathroom light. Ugly gold wall sconces—way too formal for a suburban house—flanked an equally ornate, framed mirror. She again faced her reflection.

She almost screamed but clapped a hand over her mouth and whimpered instead.

In just the few minutes it had taken her to get from her room to the bathroom, the rash had spread farther up her cheeks and down her chest.

Angel turned on the water and grabbed for soap. Maybe

if it was a rash, if she cleaned the rest of the dust and dander from her skin, it would stop any further advancement.

She started to soap up a washcloth, then she looked at her hair. Dominic had cleaned her hair, and her skin for that matter. What had been in that plastic bottle? It had been more than water . . . It had a floral smell. What if the solution in that bottle was toxic? It was from Freddy's. It wouldn't have surprised Angel at all if something was wrong with it. She needed to take a shower.

Turning off the faucet, Angel turned around to turn on the shower, and she stripped out of her clothes. She hoped everyone was sleeping deeply enough not to hear the shower. She was pretty sure they were. Even if they weren't, it didn't matter. She had to get off whatever crud she'd picked up at Freddy's.

Angel got in the marble shower and let hot water sluice over her. She reached for the shampoo and poured more over her head than she'd ever used in her life. She proceeded to scrub herself harder than she ever had. She scrubbed so hard, it hurt. And she scrubbed so hard, her skin bled. When she saw a trickle of red going down the drain, she realized she'd gone too far. She rinsed thoroughly and toweled off. She wrapped herself in another dry towel.

Before she faced the mirror again, Angel took a deep breath. "Please," she begged. "Please be better."

Closing her eyes, she moved over to the mirror. She faced it . . . and she opened her eyes. She immediately started breathing hard, almost hyperventilating. Her heart pounded out a panic rhythm of what felt like three hundred beats per minute.

Angel's legs went out from under her, and she sank down onto the fluffy white bathmat. She started to cry as her mind replayed the hideousness she'd just seen in the mirror.

The rash was on both cheeks now, and it was moving upward. It had reached the bottom of her cheekbones already. The rash was moving down, too. It covered most of her chest, and it had spread to her shoulders.

It must have gotten so fully into her system that washing did no good. What could she do now?

Angel started to put her head in her hands, but she stopped herself. What if it got on her hands, too?

Angel looked wildly around the room as if some solution to her problem was going to present itself. None did.

"What do I do?" she asked. She didn't know whom she was asking, but for some reason, she got an answer.

Angel snapped her fingers and crawled over to the vanity cabinet under the sink. She threw the doors open and began pawing through the first aid and other supplies stored there. She thought . . . yes, there it was. A few months ago, Ophelia got poison ivy, and Angel's mom bought calamine lotion. Maybe that would help.

Angel flung aside bottles and boxes in the cabinet until she could reach the bottle of pinkish liquid. She grabbed it, opened it, and began slathering herself with calamine.

When she was done, she sat on the floor and tried to calm her breathing. In through the nose—one, two, three.

Out through the mouth—one, two, three. She did this ten times and told herself everything was okay.

The itching wasn't as bad, she didn't think. That was good, right?

Angel sat and breathed some more. She could feel her heart rate slowing. *It's going to be okay*, she told herself. *Everything is fine. You just have a little rash from the stuff in that bottle . . . not that different, really, from getting a poison ivy rash.* Ophelia had survived that just fine. Angel would be fine, too.

Angel realized she was getting cold. She reached into the cabinet for a third towel.

That's when she saw that the rash could now be seen on her upper arms, well below the edge of the now-crusty calamine lotion.

"No!" Angel gasped.

She jumped up, her heart hammering again.

She looked in the mirror. Her mouth dropped open. Not only was the rash spreading well beyond where she'd put the calamine lotion, but the rash looked different now, too. Was the calamine making it worse?

Angel got back in the shower and rinsed off all the lotion. Getting out again and wrapping herself in a new towel, she forced herself to return to the mirror.

A shriek of terror caught in her throat. She started to shiver uncontrollably.

She was turning into a lizard: a slimy, squishy-looking lizard. From beneath her eyes, down her entire face and neck and chest, and now moving lower on her arms, gelatinous-looking scales were forming on her skin. The scales were red and gray and pink, and they looked moist and spongy even though she'd just dried herself off.

Angel was horrified but also unable to look away from the horror unfolding in her mirror. What was it?

She examined her arm, and she carefully touched one of the gooey scales. It felt springy, like a rubbery pillow, kind of viscous to the touch.

It felt kind of like a wet gumdrop.

Angel sucked in air.

Could this have something to do with that stupid gumdrop nose?

She closed her eyes and ground her teeth together. This was all Ophelia's fault. If she hadn't had her stupid party and gotten that stupid nose . . .

Angel could have had an allergic reaction to the nose. What was in it?

Wait. Allergic reaction. Whether it was the gumdrop nose or not that caused it, Angel could have been having an allergic reaction. That was easy enough to fix, right?

Angel turned and crossed the bathroom to the wall cabinet next to the door. This was where her mother kept over-the-counter medicines that she didn't want Ophelia getting into. Surely, they had some antihistamines.

Angel opened the cabinet door and sorted frantically through the boxes, bottles, and vials. *Yes!* Angel spotted a box of antihistamines, and she didn't even bother to read the dosage instructions. She took three of them. Then she sat on the toilet seat and waited.

She didn't know how long to wait. How long did it take for these things to start working?

She sang softly while she waited. She sang three full songs. Her eyelids started to feel heavy. Didn't antihistamines make you feel drowsy? If so, that meant the pills were working.

Excited, Angel stood to look in the mirror again.

She again had to cover her mouth so she wouldn't scream.

Her eyelids weren't heavy because she was drowsy. Her eyelids were heavy because they were now covered with the sticky scales. So was most of her forehead and the rest of her arms.

Making sure her towel was securely tucked around her, Angel grabbed her discarded clothes, slapped off the bathroom light, threw open the bathroom door, and ran down the hall toward her room as quietly as she could. She couldn't handle this on her own. She needed to get to a hospital.

She had to get dressed, and she didn't want to put on the clothes she just took off. They could be infected. She probably shouldn't even have been carrying them. But it was too late now.

As she passed her mom and Myron's room, she hesitated. She wondered if she should wake them.

No! No way. What was wrong with her? Were the gloopy scales spreading to her brain, too?

If she'd had normal parents, loving parents, of course, she'd go to them for help. But she had her useless mother, and she had Myron. She had the two people most responsible for everything wrong in her life. They were the jerks who wouldn't help her with college because they were too busy spoiling her brat of a stepsister. No way was she going to ask them for help.

In effect, she had no family. She was alone.

Angel slipped into her room and leaned back against the door. Should she call one of her friends? She didn't have what she'd call a BFF, but she hung out with a lot of kids in the drama department. One of them might help her.

As soon as she had the idea, she dismissed it. She didn't want those people to see her like this. They might help, but they'd also see her situation as an opportunity. Looking like this, she wasn't going to be able to perform the final spring performances. No, her "friends" would be more likely to gloat over her predicament than help her with it.

And what about her teachers? No. Same thing. They were supportive, but their support had a lot to do with her looks. She couldn't let them see her like this.

She saw herself in the ER all by herself . . . all by herself, but surrounded by dozens of strangers. ERs were busy places. Did she really want to be seen like this in a crowded place? Absolutely not! No, the ER wasn't the place for her.

She shouldn't go to the hospital. If something from Freddy's was causing this, there was only one thing to do. Dropping her pile of clothes, Angel carefully poked in the pockets until she found Dominic's card.

Here she'd thought he was a great guy. She should have

known better. Why did she think someone who worked at that nasty pizzeria could be a good guy?

Dominic wasn't good. He worked for the awful place that made her sick!

Well, now he was going to have to help her. She'd make him help her. And he was going to get a piece of her mind, too. What kind of crud was in Freddy's anyway? Were the food and the candy poisoned? Was the water full of toxins? Germs? Did she pick up a virus there?

Angel ran to the hallway side table and grabbed the phone. "Please be there," she breathed as she dialed Freddy's number. He did say he could always call her . . . but she also wasn't sure what time the arcade closed. It was really late.

Dominic answered on the third ring.

"Freddy Fazbear's Piz—" he began.

"What did you do to me?" Angel snapped before he could finish.

"Angel? Is that you?"

"Yes, it's me. Or at least it is for now, but I don't know how much longer I'm going to *be* me."

"I'm sorry? Can you slow down? I think I might be missing something. You're not making sense."

"What do you have in that horrible place?" She wanted to shout, but she didn't want anyone to wake up. So, she asked her question in quiet, clipped tones.

"Can we back up? I feel like I got on a train in the middle of its run. I don't know where it started, and I don't know where it's going."

"Stop trying to be clever."

"I'm not being clever. In fact, I think I'm being pretty dense. I really don't know what you're talking about. Can you please start at the beginning?"

"I should have known you weren't any different than other guys. Sure, you seemed different, but you were just playing games, weren't you? What did you do to me?"

Dominic sighed. "Angel, please tell me what's going on."

"I'm turning into a slimy, squishy, disgusting lizard is what's going on. I have these putrid scales spreading all over me!"

Angel thought she heard Dominic groan, but she didn't stop talking. "That's what's going on. And it has to have something to do with being at Freddy's today. It could have been whatever you had in that plastic bottle maybe. Or something in the food or candy. Or . . . you tell me! Something at Freddy's did this!"

Dominic was silent.

He was still on the line. Angel could hear him breathing.

"Dominic?"

Dominic still didn't speak.

"Are you there?" Angel asked.

Another few seconds passed. "I'm so sorry, Angel," he finally said.

"So you know what's wrong with me?"

"You need to come to Freddy's," he said.

"You didn't answer me."

"Come to Freddy's, and I'll explain." His voice, already so smooth and deep, dropped even lower. It soothed her. She could feel her heart rate slow just a little.

"And I'll help you, Angel. Just get to Freddy's."

Angel's fury at Dominic and the stupid pizzeria abated enough for her to feel a spark of hope. "You'll help me?" Her voice sounded small, but she didn't care.

"Yes, I'll help you. Just come here to Freddy's."

"Okay."

"And, Angel?"

"Yeah?"

"Hurry."

"Okay."

"Bye."

Angel hesitated for just an instant, then said, "Bye."

Angel sat on the floor for several seconds clutching the phone and listening to the dead air of the ended call. Dominic would help her. And maybe he hadn't betrayed her after all.

Maybe everything would be okay.

Angel suddenly realized how much time she was wasting. She dropped the phone, jumped up, and ran back to her room.

Angel yanked open bureau drawers and pulled out fresh underwear, a bra, jeans, and a T-shirt. She threw on her clothes as fast as she could, and she thrust her feet into her sandals.

Okay, that was the easy part. Now she had to get to Freddy's.

She couldn't walk. It was too far. Not to mention, she didn't want to be seen.

She looked at the digital clock on her nightstand. It was

11:35 p.m.—dark, but it wasn't late enough for the streets to be totally deserted.

She thought about biking, but even that would take her a long time. No. The dreadful jelly-scales were spreading too fast. She needed to drive. She'd take her mother's sports car. She'd driven the car plenty of times. Sometimes, when Myron wasn't around, her mom would tell Angel she wanted to go on a drive and she felt like being chauffeured. Angel loved driving the zippy car. She wished it were hers.

So driving the car wasn't an issue, but getting it away from the house might be. Could she deactivate the alarm, get into the garage, open the garage door, start the car, and leave without anyone waking up?

She had to. She had to get this handled or her life was going to be totally ruined.

Angel grabbed one of her scarves and wrapped it around her head so it would obscure her face as much as possible. She tucked her hair behind her ears.

Suddenly, Angel thought of the way Dominic had tucked her hair behind her ear. Her eyes filled with tears. It figured. Story of her life. *I meet an amazing guy and I start turning into a clammy reptile*, she thought.

Would Dominic still like her when he saw the way she looked now? Was he as one-dimensional as all the other guys she'd met—the ones whose interest only went skin-deep? If he was, that was the end of it. Even if he wasn't, how could they go out with her looking like this? How long would it take for this to go away? Would it be gone by graduation? By the time she left for the summer workshop?

Why couldn't things go Angel's way for a change? It really wasn't fair.

By the time Angel got into her mother's bright yellow sports car, the squidgy reptile skin had completely covered Angel's arms. She assumed it was heading down her legs, too, because they felt funny. Her stomach felt strange as well, kind of heavy. She noticed that when she sat down in the driver's seat of the car; she was shorter in the seat than she ever had been before. She had to adjust the rearview mirror downward, and she usually had to adjust it upward because she was a little taller than her mom.

When she noticed this, she lifted her shirt to see what was happening. She let out a little scream. Her stomach had gotten so elastic that it was kind of collapsing in on itself when she sat down.

Was she going to be able to get to Freddy's before she was too pliable to do anything at all?

Angel backed down her driveway and pressed the button to close the garage door. Her neighborhood was an expanse of darkness broken up by outdoor porch lights. In the distance, a dog barked, but otherwise, the only sound was the car's engine. None of the houses near hers had lights in the windows. It didn't look like anyone was staying up late to see Angel taking her mother's car out for a spin. Good.

Angel pointed the car in the direction of Freddy's, and she resisted the urge to stomp on the accelerator. Speeding through town wasn't the thing to do right now. So she drove, well, like an angel—careful to obey every traffic law so as not to draw any attention to herself. Being in the highly visible expensive car made being unobtrusive a little challenging even under normal circumstances, and these weren't normal circumstances.

Most of the trip was quiet and uneventful, but a block from Freddy's she had a scare. Waiting at a red light, she heard the grumble of some kind of muscle car come up next to the sports car. She didn't look over, but the driver of the car whistled and called out, "Want to have some fun, honey?"

Angel clutched the steering wheel harder. Or she tried to. When she couldn't get the grip she wanted, she looked down to see why.

Oh no!

Her fingers were turning into segmented chunks of mucous-like material that turned her stomach. They didn't even look human anymore.

The driver in the car next to hers called out again, and she glanced at the driver's door to be sure the locks were engaged. She also lowered her hands to the bottom of the steering wheel so the driver couldn't see them in the relentless intrusion of the streetlights.

The guy in the muscle car kept up a rude, suggestive patter while the light stayed red. What was taking so long for it to change?

Eventually, it turned green. The muscle car sped off. Angel let out her pent-up breath. She drove the rest of the way to Freddy's without encountering another vehicle.

When Angel finally pulled her mom's little sports car

into the parking spot closest to the front door of Freddy's, she looked around at the brightly lit lot. Thankfully, no other cars were in it. She was alone.

Now, scanning the area again, she opened the driver's door and headed toward Freddy's entrance. Before she got there, Dominic opened the door and looked out at her.

Angel's steps faltered. Even though she needed Dominic's help, she still didn't want him to see her this way. She looked down and let her hair fall forward over her face.

"Angel?" Dominic called out. "It's okay. Don't worry about how you look. I don't care about that. I just need you to hurry so I can help you."

Angel glanced at Dominic through the veil of her hair. His expression was somber. His lips were pressed together, and his eyes looked red. Had he been crying?

He really seemed to care. This made Angel trust him even more. She walked forward and put her malformed hand in his strong, perfect one.

Without any comment about her hand or any of the rest of her, he led her into Freddy's. "Come on. I'll take you to the back."

Angel let Dominic pull her down the hall. She looked up. The place looked much different now than it had a few hours ago. Not just because it was empty and quiet but because . . . because why?

Angel frowned. Was it the lighting?

During the party, every light in the restaurant had been on. Now, most of them were out, and the ones that were on were turned down to a dim setting. Every bright color in the place was muted. Shadows stretched down the hall ahead of her and created pockets of darkness along the walls and the ceiling. The effect was sobering, maybe even a little scary.

Taking a few tentative steps down the hall with Dominic, Angel could still see the pictures of the characters on the walls, but they looked less friendly now. Why was that? Was it the shadows? Or something else?

Angel took a few more steps until she heard a weird clinking sound. Suddenly scared for no good reason, she stopped.

"It's okay," Dominic said. "It's just one of the animatronics doing daily maintenance."

Angel nodded and began hobbling forward again.

She was feeling woozy. The edges of her vision started to get fuzzy, and her balance wavered.

Was the restaurant getting darker? No, it was the same. The problem was her—she was starting to lose consciousness.

"Dominic? I'm having trouble seeing."

Dominic put his arm around her and started moving her more quickly along the hall. He said something to her, but she didn't understand it. Something was wrong with her hearing now, too. It felt like she had cotton in her ears.

And she was sinking toward the floor. Her legs were going limp. They wouldn't hold her up anymore.

"Dominic, help me!"

Dominic lifted her into his arms, and he began trotting down the hall.

Suddenly, the lights were brighter—not by a lot but a

little—they didn't seem to reveal any of the surroundings, though. Angel's diminished vision was worsening even more. The walls and floors going past her were taking on an amorphous quality; they were losing their edges and becoming indistinct, almost impressionistic.

Angel tried to blink and bring a hand up to wipe her eyes, but her arms just swung loose at her sides. She couldn't get them to respond to her brain's commands.

But really, what *were* her brain's commands? Her brain was meandering around as if her brain cells had turned into soft rubber. No, not rubber. She sensed they were turning into goo, like that goopy clay stuff Ophelia liked to play with, smooshing it between her little fingers like melting cheese oozing out of a grilled cheese sandwich.

"Okay, Angel. We're here. I'm going to put you in something that's going to help you. Do you understand?"

Angel nodded because she could suddenly hear again. Why?

Maybe it was the relief. She was getting the help she needed. Dominic knew what was going on. He said he'd explain it. He hadn't explained, and she wanted him to; but mostly, she just wanted him to make it stop.

Maybe Dominic has an antilope. No, that isn't right. Antidote. That's what it is.

She tried to talk again, but she couldn't.

She could see again, though. Like her hearing, her eyesight had miraculously cleared up. She blinked, and she could clearly see that Dominic was getting ready to lower her into a box. It was such a pretty box, a shiny wood box, its grain so swirly and lovely that Angel wanted to become part of the box. She wanted the box to embrace her, hold her, and keep her safe.

As soon as she saw the box, Angel no longer cared about what was happening to her. She didn't care about why it was happening, either. She didn't need an explanation. She was where she was supposed to be.

Dominic bent over and began to put Angel in the box, and she tried to speak again. She wanted to say thank you. All she could get out was "Th-u."

"I know. I know," Dominic said. "It's going to be okay." His voice sounded odd, broken, like he was crying.

Angel felt moisture on her forehead when Dominic leaned over her. Tears. She wanted to tell him it was okay. She was in the box now. It was her box. It belonged to her, and she belonged to it.

Angel felt something prying at her eyes and her mouth. She felt hands prodding the skin on her arms.

"It's okay, Angel," Dominic repeated. "It will be just a few hours at most."

A few hours until what? Angel hoped it was a few hours until she was all well. Wouldn't that be great? She had something she wanted to do. What was it?

"I'm here, Angel," Dominic said. "You're not alone."

Dominic! That was what she wanted to do! She wanted to go out with Dominic. If she was better in a few hours, she'd be able to go.

Where were they going to go?

"Do you feel anything?" Dominic asked.

Angel wanted to answer that question. Yes, she felt things. She felt a hard surface beneath her body. She felt something cool under her head. She felt the warmth of the bright light shining down on her. She felt hands on her forehead.

"Close your eyes, Angel," Dominic said.

Angel did what he told her to do. The light went away. The world went dark. She could still hear, but sounds were distorted, like she was floating in water, her ears just below the surface.

"There you go," Dominic said. "It will be over soon."

Good, Angel thought, and she let unconsciousness take her.

Angel woke up abruptly, as if someone poked her or shouted at her. She was fully alert. That was good, wasn't it?

She had a vague memory of being really out of it before she went to sleep. The rash had done something to her thinking.

The rash!

Did she still have it?

Angel tried to sit up.

She couldn't. She couldn't move at all.

What was going on?

She tried again. It felt like she was paralyzed.

Not liking that feeling at all, Angel writhed, and hit her forehead on something hard. She squirmed some more, and her elbows and knees whacked something hard.

Not paralyzed. Confined.

In what?

For several moments, Angel fought to get free of the box she was in. She lamented Ophelia's party, which she understood vaguely was responsible for where she was now.

But then she stopped struggling.

Angel told herself to stay calm. Take stock. Then figure out what to do next.

She scanned her body. It felt foreign, not familiar at all. But she could sense that she seemed to be in an upright position. She was standing? If she was, she was standing in some kind of a box that was so tightly fit around her that she had no leeway to move.

Angel's breathing quickened. She didn't like confined spaces.

She opened her mouth to call out, but her mouth was covered with something. Tape? She couldn't get her lips to part. She couldn't feel her teeth, either. And she was having a little trouble breathing. Her nose felt funny, like it was partially plugged with something.

Angel was on the verge of panic when, suddenly, she felt space open up beneath her feet. Then she felt the sensation of being lowered. Down, down, down.

From what seemed like a great distance, she could hear the sound of children screaming. She recoiled. She hated the sound of children screaming. That sound always reminded her of her bothersome stepsister, Ophelia.

Over the sound of the screaming, Angel heard a musical fanfare and a booming announcer's voice. She couldn't make out all his words, but it sounded like he was talking about someone's birthday. And she heard, "Grand finale."

Why did those words seem familiar?

The children's screams turned into cheers and laughter, and Angel's eyes were suddenly assaulted by bright, bright lights and lots of dazzling colors. She tried to figure out where she was because she had the sense she'd been here before, recently. But all she could see was light and color.

The sensation of being lowered stopped, and now Angel could feel that she was hanging in midair. She felt her body swaying back and forth, back and forth. It was not a pleasant sensation, so she tried to control the motion by twisting herself this way and that. She also flailed her arms, and she was pleasantly surprised that she could. She was hanging, but at least she was no longer confined. She kicked out her legs, and she flexed her hands and feet.

The announcer was saying something else. Angel caught the word *yummy* but she couldn't work out the rest of what was being said.

The children's clamor was getting louder, though. It felt like they were getting closer, too. Angel felt like she was being surrounded.

She moved her body around some more, doing a sort of midair dance. She wondered if she could do a somersault. She tried. No. Something was attached to the top of her head.

The announcer spoke again. His words were all run together, all mushy, until he got to his last three words. Angel heard those clearly: "Ready, set, go!"

Julie smiled up at the announcer when he said, "Ready, set, go!" She took a step toward the gummy girl oscillating from the ceiling. She so liked being the center of attention that she wanted to stretch out the moment.

She turned to look out at her parents. They beamed at her. She waved to them.

"Happy birthday, Julie!" her mom called out.

"Yay, birthday girl!" her dad shouted.

Julie grinned, and she leaned over to the gummy girl dangling in front of her. She reached up a hand, grabbed the foot, and bit off the gummy's big toe.

"Everyone, join in!" the announcer sang out.

The other kids crowded around Julie, and they began eating up the swaying, squirming gummy candy that was unlike any other.

Sergio looked up from his drafting board and squinted in annoyance at the bright sunshine blasting through the wall-to-wall windows along the front of the office building. He shifted to avoid being blinded, and he rubbed at the afternoon kink in his neck. He checked the time on his new stainless-steel, aviator-style watch: 2:32 p.m. He peered at the sub-dials within the main dial of the watch. His watch had three sub-dials, and he had no use for any of them, but they looked impressive. And things that looked impressive made him feel impressive.

Above all, that was what Sergio wanted to be: impressive.

"I keep telling you, you have to be careful what you wish for, Serge."

Sergio jerked toward the man who'd come up behind him, and he knocked over his coffee mug in the process. It went flying, but the man, Dale, Sergio's supervisor, caught it. Dale was a senior manager in their architectural firm and a big guy, an ex-football player, to boot. The mug looked puny in his massive hand.

"Now you've gone and done it," Dale said, flicking a few drops of coffee from his wrist. Thankfully there wasn't much left in the mug. The sun hit the top of Dale's shaved head, and it shined so bright it looked like a halo.

"Sorry, Dale. Didn't mean to throw a mug at you."

"What?" Dale looked down at the mug, then thrust it back at Sergio. "Forget the mug. You got it, Serge. You got the project manager job."

Sergio stood, then grinned. "Really? I thought the decision wasn't going to be made until next week."

"It got pushed up because Sanders is leaving sooner than we thought he was."

Sergio slid his shiny black wingtips over the gray carpet in an abbreviated moonwalk back toward the sunshine behind him. Then he twirled and did a fist pump.

Dale chuckled. "Congratulations." He held out his hand.

Sergio shook his hand, but then he frowned. "What did you mean by what you said?"

"What did I say?"

"Well, you said two things: *Be careful what you wish for* and *Now you've gone and done it.*"

"Well, you do realize how hard project managers work, right? Are you ready to start living at the office?"

Sergio laughed.

Dale didn't.

Sergio sobered. "Are you serious?"

Dale grinned and punched Sergio's arm. "Only a little. You'll probably only have to sleep here three or four nights a month."

Sergio nodded as if that was just fine, but it really wasn't.

The truth was that when he applied for the project manager job, he hadn't really been thinking about what the job would be like. He applied because it was the next logical step up from where he was. He was on a fast track to the top, and staying on that track meant applying for promotions, whether you wanted to do more work or not.

At twenty-seven, he'd defied the laws of becoming an architect to get to where he already was. He got through the college and post-grad work needed by the time he was twenty-one. He was hired by the best architectural firm in town and had his license by the time he was twenty-two. It only took him three years to get to senior architect, much to the annoyance of several older architects who got passed over. And now he was the firm's youngest ever project manager.

Why was he able to do all of this? Well, one, he was an architectural phenom—ever since he was a kid, he had a head for numbers and an eye for spatial relationships. He knew how to mold physical reality into something eye-catching. And two, he was determined. He was so determined to reach the top that he willed himself to work as hard as he had to; nothing would stop him from getting what he wanted.

But, lately, he'd begun to wonder whether what he wanted was really what he wanted.

"Earth to Serge," Dale said. "Lost you there."

Sergio shook his head. "Sorry."

"Don't worry," Dale said. "We won't make you sleep here tonight." Dale let loose with one of his full laughs, which was just one step below a sonic boom.

Sergio noticed that not a single head on the design floor lifted at the sound. Everyone was used to it.

Dale tapped Sergio's drafting desk. "I'll let you get back to it, but after work we should go out for dinner to celebrate your promotion. Say, seven thirty? Oh, and you'll need to pack up your stuff. I'll have janitorial bring you boxes. They'll be moving your things into your office tomorrow."

Sergio smiled. That was another reason he'd applied for the project manager job: He was going to get his own office, an enclosed space. No more working out here in the open with the other junior and senior architects. Now, that was impressive.

As soon as Dale strode away, Sergio's closest work buddy—both in terms of desk location and time spent together—Clive, threw a wadded-up piece of paper at him. "Congrats, you idiot."

Sergio deflected the ball of paper and said, "You're just jealous."

"Not even a little, Idiot." Clive shook his round head, and his bushy brown hair flew into his eyes.

For at least the thousandth time, Sergio marveled at how much his friend looked like Bubbles, the chocolate labradoodle Clive and his girlfriend, Fiona, another architect in the firm, doted on. It wasn't just Clive's brown curly hair. It was his big brown eyes, the earthy tones he dressed in, and the fluid way he moved, always ready for some kind of fun. Once, Sergio told Clive that he looked like Bubbles, and Clive responded with "Yeah, well you look like Trotter."

Sergio had to laugh at that. Trotter was Dale's dog, a spoiled miniature pinscher, and Sergio actually could see the resemblance. Like Trotter, he was small and compact and slender, and he had a somewhat pointed nose. Also like Trotter, though, he was muscular and sleek. He wore his black hair slicked back, and he always dressed in dark, fitted clothing. He knew he wasn't good-looking, but he did his best to have his own impressive (of course) style. And his girlfriend, Violet, a junior architect at the firm, didn't seem to mind how he looked.

"You realize I'm your boss now," Sergio reminded Clive.

Clive snorted. "Fine. Mr. Idiot."

Sergio grinned, shook his head, and tried to concentrate on his work.

Most of the department came to Sergio's promotion dinner. Considering it was short notice for everyone, Sergio thought that was impressive. He hoped it was because he was well liked and not because they were sucking up. But he couldn't tell. He could never tell with people. He couldn't read people, not even Violet, whom he'd been dating for almost a year. He was often unsure about what she was really thinking. Did she mean it when she said he was awesome, or was she dating him because he was moving up in the firm, and she thought he'd take her with him?

That was why he had to rely on hard work to get him the life he wanted. He was never going to schmooze his way to the top. He could no more schmooze than he could slam-dunk a basketball.

The dinner wasn't anything fancy. They all just traipsed across the street to the steakhouse that had been a fixture on the block well before the firm moved into their new office building the year before. But that was okay. The steakhouse had great food, and it had the kind of old-world atmosphere Sergio liked—wood-paneled walls, leather chairs, dark-stained tables, plush gold carpeting, and ornate wall sconces.

Dale had reserved the restaurant's meeting room, and

now Sergio sat at a round table filled with his fellow architects—twelve of the fourteen in his department were here. Everyone was having a great time—joking, laughing, flirting.

Strike that. Everyone *but* Sergio was having a great time.

Yes, he was throwing out one-liners and laughing at the right times, but his heart wasn't in it. Ever since he'd gotten the news of his promotion, he'd been battling a sudden onset of depression he couldn't explain. What was wrong with him? He'd gotten good news, but it didn't feel good at all.

"So what's it like to be the new project manager?" Violet asked as Sergio cut into his medium-rare rib eye.

The grilled aroma of the beef on his plate combined with savory scents of butter and onions. His mouth watered as he watched pink juices run from the steak. He speared the bite he'd just cut apart.

Sergio looked at his freckled, brunette girlfriend. Short and pillowy, Violet was the picture of curvy femininity. To play up her soft features, Violet wore clothes with lots of trim and ruffles and color. Her wardrobe had "sass," as she called it. She was always asking him if she looked sassy. He wasn't sure how sassy looked, so he always said, "You look sassy as heck, babe." Basically, he lied.

Looking at Violet now, Sergio realized he often lied when it came to Violet.

"Don't you just love romantic comedies?" Violet had asked just the other night as they headed to the theater for yet another romantic comedy movie.

"Sure do, babe," Sergio said. He hated romantic comedies. Give him a good sci-fi or supernatural movie any day. Even horror was better than a romantic comedy.

"I hate horror movies," Violet had said on their second date. "Don't you?"

"Absolutely," Sergio said.

The same kind of thing happened with food. "Everyone seems to love Chinese food," Violet said on their third date. "But I don't get the appeal. It's either too bland or too spicy. What do you think?"

"I totally agree," Sergio said. Chinese takeout was one of his favorite things.

Violet chose how they spent their time, too.

On their first date, Violet announced that she was a "go-getter." She let Sergio know that quiet nights at home would be rare. "My mama always said, 'You stand still too long, Vi, and you'll sprout roots. You gotta keep rolling so you don't gather moss.' So I like to keep moving, keep doing. When I'm not at work, I'm out having fun. You know?"

Sergio had nodded even though he was still untangling her mixed metaphors and he really liked hanging out at home. "Sure," he said. "Life's too short to grow moss on your roots."

Violet thought that was hilariously funny, which was nice because he liked it when people found his attempts at humor amusing. But it was equally not nice because Violet had a truly obnoxious laugh. A cross between a honk, a siren, and a snore, Violet's laugh attracted attention the way syrup attracted flies. She'd embarrassed Sergio on dozens of occasions. He actually started trying *not* to be amusing. It didn't work. Apparently he was the master of inadvertently saying funny things. Like just this evening. After Dale told him about the promotion, Sergio went to Violet's drafting table and told her the good news. "There'll be a dinner tonight. I assume you want to come?" She'd laughed as if he'd just told the best joke ever. He found that baffling.

Yes, Violet was smart, and yes, they had shared interests, and yes, she was pretty fun. But was it really so much to want a girlfriend who liked more of the things he liked? He wondered if they'd still be dating if he'd told her the truth from the beginning.

Would she even like him if she knew him, *really* knew him? Heck, sometimes he wasn't sure if she liked the version of him that he was pretending to be.

And sometimes he didn't like her much, either. Violet was a flirt. Even though she was with Sergio, she liked to come on to other men. And not just some men. *All* men. Married or unmarried. She didn't care. She just liked to flirt.

Sergio had never liked the flirting, but lately it was really getting on his nerves.

"Sergio?"

Sergio blinked and looked at Violet.

She was tugging on his sleeve. "I asked you a question."

"I'm sorry. What did you ask?"

"I asked you how it feels to be the new project manager."

Waiting until he'd put his first bite of steak in his mouth and chewed it, Sergio gave Violet what he hoped was a neutral look that didn't betray his annoyance at her. For once, he gave her an honest answer. "Well, I'm not the project manager yet, am I? So, I don't know."

Violet let loose with her laugh.

Sergio looked down and quickly took another bite of steak.

The biggest issue in his relationship was that . . . well, Violet wasn't the girl he really wanted. But *that* girl was someone he hadn't seen in years. He wondered what she was doing now.

Sophia Manchester started going to Sergio's high school during his junior year. He fell in love with her on the first day she came to class. Small and graceful like a ballerina, Sophia had the dark looks he loved, and she had the face of an angel. She was also very smart, very nice, very funny . . . and, unfortunately, very popular. Although she was always perfectly kind to him and he'd noticed she seemed to like a lot of the same things he liked, they moved in entirely different circles. He didn't stand a chance.

But he never forgot her. In the nearly ten years since he'd seen her, he'd been trying to find a woman like her. Violet, sadly, wasn't that woman.

Violet patted his leg, then turned away from him to flirt with Clive even though only an airhead would flirt with Clive. Everyone knew Clive was obviously taken by out-spoken, red-haired Fiona, who sat on his other side now, and Fiona was not a woman to be messed with.

Case in point: When Violet leaned toward Clive to rub her chest against his arm, a spoonful of Fiona's mashed potatoes flew across the table and onto Violet's new blouse.

"Oh sorry," Fiona purred in her smooth, confident voice. "I don't know how that got away from me."

Violet sniffed loudly, and extricated the potatoes from her blouse. She leaned away from Clive.

Sergio suppressed a smile and concentrated on his steak. The steak was the best part of this evening's celebration. He could have done without the forced camaraderie. Being friendly with other people was hard work, and he was tired tonight. He wanted to go home and stop trying for just a few hours.

But he couldn't do that yet. He had to keep eating and bantering and pretending all was right in the world.

After most of the plates on the table had been cleared away by the waiters, Dale stood and tapped his water glass.

The *ding-ding-ding* brought up every head at the table.

"So, Serge," Dale said, "we want a speech. You know we do."

Everyone except Clive started chanting, "Speech, speech, speech." Clive was mouthing *Idiot* at Sergio.

Sergio smiled and stood. "I'll make this short and sweet."

Everyone cheered. Dale laughed. "See? There's a reason this kid has advanced so quickly."

Sergio grinned, as he knew he was supposed to. "Well, here we go. Thank you, Dale, to you and the partners, for the promotion."

Dale inclined his head, smiling. "You deserve it."

Sergio smiled. "And to the rest of you"—he lowered his voice to a growl—"you're mine now, maggots. And don't you forget it." He sat down.

The table was silent for at least three seconds, then Clive burst out laughing and started clapping. Violet joined in, and then everyone was laughing. *Whew.* For a second, Sergio thought he'd blown it.

Of course, Violet wanted to go out dancing after the dinner, and she convinced Sergio to invite Clive and Fiona and a couple other architects. Even though Sergio enjoyed showing off his dance moves, they stayed up ridiculously late. Finally, Sergio took Violet home and then headed to his own apartment building a few blocks away.

Pulling his two-year-old SUV into his assigned space in the garage under his apartment building, Sergio picked up his suit jacket from the leather passenger seat. He stepped out of the black vehicle, then closed and locked the doors. For a few seconds, he stood and stared at his SUV.

He remembered how excited he was when he bought it. He'd been wanting to trade in his old small pickup for a nice SUV for years. Once he'd done it, though, he realized he still didn't have the vehicle he truly desired. Why was it that whenever he climbed a little higher on the ladder, he felt like he still had too many rungs to go before he reached the top?

Sighing, Sergio left his SUV behind him and took the elevator to the third floor. There, he strode to his apartment, hurrying quietly with his back to his neighbor's door. Mrs. Bailey was a busybody, and she liked to ambush him when he got home. Only once in a while did he manage to get past—

"Oh, it's just you, Sergio," Mrs. Bailey's scratchy voice said as Sergio put his key in his lock. "I thought I heard an intruder. You're quite late tonight. Hot date?"

Sergio took a breath, then turned. "Hi, Mrs. Bailey."

The petite, gray-haired lady beamed at him. In the daytime she usually wore crisply ironed shirtdresses in pastel colors, but tonight she was sporting a frilly pink nightgown under a white quilted robe. "How was work today?"

"Fine." Sergio wasn't going to tell her about the promotion. Oh, no. She would have insisted on inviting him in for some kind of baked good, in spite of the time. He yawned, not a fake yawn, just a well-timed one. "I'm awfully tired, Mrs. Bailey. Please forgive me, but I need to get inside and go to bed."

"Of course you do, dear." Mrs. Bailey smiled at him. "You go get your rest."

Sergio thanked his lucky stars and slipped into his apartment before Mrs. Bailey could say anything else. He closed the door behind him and latched all four latches.

He leaned back against his door and closed his eyes. Home at last.

Sergio had a nice apartment. At 1,200 square feet, it was far from tiny, and the complex had been built only two years before. It sported the most up-to-date appliances and modern features that his architectural eye appreciated.

A couple friends from the firm had helped Sergio decorate his apartment, and it looked good. They'd used neutral beiges and grays that felt both upscale and masculine, and most of the furnishings were expensive antiques. It was a decent place, but he resented that it was in a building that also housed the likes of Mrs. Bailey. He deserved peace, didn't he? He shouldn't have to put up with a nosy old lady who didn't have anything better to do than torment him.

Sergio crossed the living room and went into his bedroom. Removing his wallet from his pocket, he placed it in the ceramic tray he used for his wallet and keys and whatever other detritus might come out of his pockets at the end of the day. He then undressed and carefully hung up his suit and put everything else in a laundry hamper. Tugging on gray sweats and a black T-shirt, he lay down on the bed and dropped immediately into sleep.

The next morning, his alarm woke him at 6:00 a.m. Feeling groggy and foggy, he groaned and turned on the TV. Flipping through the channels, he thought about the long day he had ahead. He should get moving.

He looked at the phone on his Queen Anne cherry nightstand. He checked his watch. It wasn't too early. He picked up the phone.

Leaning back on a pile of gray, white, and beige pillows, Sergio listened to the phone ring. It was picked up on the third one.

"Hello?" his mother's lightly accented voice said.

"Mama," Sergio said.

"Sergio! What a nice surprise!" Something rustled

against the phone, and her voice was muffled as she called, "Tony! Come here. It's Sergio on the phone." Her voice returned to full volume and beyond when she shouted into the phone, "Sergio? You still there? I'm putting you on speaker. Your papa is doing his morning workout. Tony! Come here! Come talk to Sergio on the speaker."

Sergio shook his head. His mother sure did love her speakerphone.

"How's our Sergio?" a deep voice boomed into the phone. "Have you built any skyscrapers lately?" The machine gun laugh that came after this ridiculous question was joined by his mother's wild giggling.

Sergio shook his head again. "You know I don't build skyscrapers, Papa. I'm in the residential renovation department of the firm."

"So renovate skyscraper apartment buildings."

"In a town where the tallest building is ten stories high?"

"You have to be a visionary, son, if you want it all. You can't reach the top without being able to *see* the top. You have to be bold and daring to stand out."

Tony Altieri knew all about being bold and daring and being on the top. The head of a massive transportation company, Sergio's dad was one impressive man. By the time Sergio was born, when Tony was thirty, Tony had already built his empire and a mansion for his wife and new baby. Since then, his business only continued to grow. Today, he not only filled his mansion with the best furniture and art and cars, but he also bought more houses to fill with furniture, art, and cars.

"I got a promotion today," Sergio said. "The one I told you I applied for . . . I got it."

"Head of the company?" Tony asked, laughing again.

"Tony, be nice," Sergio's mother said. "Congratulations, Sergio. We're so proud of you! We need to have a celebration. Your favorite pasta. And cake. We have to have cake. What was the job you applied for again?"

"Project manager."

"That sounds nice," his mother said.

Tony snorted. "Don't rest on your laurels, Sergio. Always upward. Did you catch the game last night?"

Sergio noticed he was gritting his teeth, and he forced himself to relax. "I saw the score. I missed the game because we all went out to dinner to celebrate my promotion."

"Did you meet anyone?" Sergio's mother asked.

"No, Mama. It was just the people in my department. Violet is the only woman there who's interested in me."

"They got no taste," Tony said. "At least Violet knows a good thing when she sees it."

Sergio's mother snorted. She wasn't Violet's biggest fan.

Sergio made his excuses to get off the phone as fast as he could. He was asking himself why he called his parents to begin with.

Well, he knew why he called them: He called them to get validation. He was trying to feel like he'd finally gotten enough to have "arrived." Why in the world did he think he'd get that validation from his father?

All the rich food he ate the night before must have slowed down his brain function.

Sergio's new office was outstanding. His new job was not.

The office wasn't huge; it wasn't a corner office or anything. Honestly, it was just a small plain room tucked between the break room and a conference room, but it was his. Plus his windows had shades, which for some reason were missing from the windows out on the design floor. Sergio happily pulled those shades down when the sun came around to spear his eyes at two in the afternoon.

The shade-pulling moment was, however, the only happy moment of the day. The rest of the day was just a mind-numbing blur as he tried to get up to speed with what Sanders had been doing . . . or rather, had *not* been doing. After just two hours of assessing the situation, he understood why Sanders had left earlier than expected. This was not a job for one person. It was a job for at least ten people, plus assistants. Clive was right. Sergio was an idiot.

He hadn't been told what his pay raise would be before he applied for the promotion, but he figured it would be a decent increase. He was wrong. He was only going to get another $1,000 a month. To do ten times more work.

"Idiot," he muttered to himself as he tried to organize the few tasks he thought he might be able to get done today . . . if he stayed until nearly midnight.

Sergio's door opened, and Clive's head popped in, along with the aromas wafting over from the break room. Sergio could smell coffee, popcorn, and someone's microwaved burritos.

"How's the new job?" Clive asked.

Sergio dropped his head to the pile of paperwork in front of him and pounded it a couple times.

"That good, huh?" Clive came the rest of the way into the room and sat in one of the narrow leather and stainless-steel chairs in front of Sergio. He looked around at Sergio's plain oak desk, the other chair, the shelves piled with project files, and the drafting table tucked in the corner.

"So you *do* have a drafting table," Clive noted. "Think you'll get to use it?"

Sergio didn't answer the question. Instead he asked, "Do you ever think we reach our ideals?"

Clive turned sideways and put his feet up on the other chair in front of the desk. "That's a deep question."

"Sorry. I know you hate to use your dozen or so brain cells to think about deep questions."

"Yeah. You're stressing me out here."

"Never mind."

"No, it's a good question. Honest answer? I don't think ideals are actually real. I think they exist only in our heads. I mean, have you ever drawn something that was as good as you imagined it in your head? If you have, I'll buy you dinner every night for a week, because I sure haven't."

"As tempting as it is to lie to get those dinners," Sergio said, grinning, "no, I haven't."

"There you go. We're all a bunch of donkeys."

"What?"

"You know. The carrot and the stick. We're just a bunch of donkeys plodding along trying to reach a carrot that will forever dangle out in front of us, no matter how far we plod."

"That's depressing."

Clive shrugged and shook his head, doing an unintentional impression of Bubbles the labradoodle. "Then my work is done." He grinned. "Seriously, I don't think it's depressing at all. It's kind of freeing when you think about it. If we can't ever get what we want, why bother trying? Just do your best and have a good time." He paused and saluted. "Mr. Idiot, sir." He bowed multiple times as he backed out of Sergio's office.

Sergio laughed, then sobered and tried to concentrate on work.

Two and a half weeks into the new position, Sergio had doubled his caffeine consumption, and still he was constantly ten paces behind. He'd already made two dumb mistakes that cost the firm several thousand dollars, and he'd already been berated twice by a client. Dale assured him this was a normal part of the learning curve for the project manager's job, but Sergio was still mortified.

He was also bored and disappointed. He'd thought that becoming the project manager would give him more leeway to implement cutting-edge design ideas, more freedom to break past the boundaries of the usual renovations his department did. For some time, he was frustrated by the safe, limited changes their clients made to their homes.

He wanted to be given carte blanche to bust into a place, demo the heck out of it, and turn it into something else entirely. He thought a project manager would hold enough sway that he could make that vision a reality. He was wrong. The projects he had to oversee were the same old things, and now, in addition to disliking the types of jobs he was working on, he had responsibility for more aspects of those jobs. This new position really was just more work and no more satisfaction.

Not only was work in full suck mode, but his home life, such as it was, had gone down the toilet as well. Mrs. Bailey had taken to staying up late so she could greet him with her latest suggestions for getting more sleep.

Then there was the tenant who lived above him. The woman who had the apartment on the next floor up took dancing lessons. He'd been listening to her stomping around above his head for weeks. He didn't know her name, but he'd given her the title of "Thunder Feet." Now, for some reason, Thunder Feet was practicing until 2:00 a.m. He tried to talk to her about it one night, but after scolding *him* for ringing her doorbell too late, she called him names that made him blush.

Also, because he never had time to go to the grocery store, he was eating more takeout, and because he was so tired when he got home, he rarely exercised and instead just dropped into bed. These two changes had resulted in a disturbing potbelly that was growing with each passing day.

Sergio's dissatisfaction was growing with each passing

day, too. So were the number of hours he was working. It was near midnight most nights when he left the firm, and he always came home with a stack of work to look over before he went to bed.

As if all this wasn't bad enough, Violet hated Sergio's new long hours even more than he did. And it was turning her into a nag.

"How come you have to work all the time, Sergio?" she asked him on Saturday night, at the end of his first week as project manager. They were at a party she insisted they attend even though they couldn't get there until after 10:30 p.m. because he worked until then. He knew she was going to want to stay until at least two or later, and then he was going to have to get up and go into work early Sunday morning. If he didn't, there was no way he could handle Monday.

"Um, because it's part of the new job?" Sergio said with a thick layer of sarcasm. "The new job I just got promoted into. It's a high-workload job. What do you suggest I do? Get a saw and cut the workload in half?"

He never should have said that. Violet laughed hysterically, and everyone at the party turned to stare at them.

And so it went. Work. Try and please his girlfriend. Get home late. Deal with Mrs. Bailey. Eat junk. Listen to Thunder Feet. Finally go to sleep. Rinse and repeat.

His days were basically drudgery. The only few minutes in them that he really liked were those moments when he walked out of the building, admired his dedicated project manager's parking spot (now there was a perk worth working your tail off for . . . not!), strolled to it, and got in his car. That was his fleeting moment of freedom. Every night—he got just a few seconds of joy in the feeling of escape.

But even that was beyond his reach on this rainy Tuesday night.

Because the forecast had been for the usual sunshine, Sergio wasn't prepared for rain. Even though his new parking spot was only twenty feet from the firm's door, he and his stack of papers were soaked when he got into his SUV. And he was cold. And he was hungry.

Sergio put his papers on the passenger seat. He turned on the heat full blast, which caused the vehicle to steam up. And his wool suit started smelling like a wet farm animal. Or was that his own smell? He didn't know. Personal hygiene was another thing this job was taking from him.

Pulling out of the parking lot, Sergio couldn't help but notice he had the road mostly to himself. It had been like that every night this week . . . which was why it was not just annoying but screamingly inconvenient when his two-year-old SUV decided to die in the totally closed-down and deserted retail district of downtown. Sergio was barely able to coast to the curb before the SUV lost all momentum and drifted to a full, silent stop.

Sergio looked at the still-bright dashboard lights. Not the battery. He looked at the gas tank. It was half full. Not out of gas.

"Are you kidding me?" Sergio asked his vehicle.

It had no response.

He tried to restart the SUV. Nothing. There was no point in him looking under the hood. He knew nothing about vehicle engines.

So, Sergio sat in the dead SUV and listened to rain thrumming on the roof. He tried to see through the gray murk of the falling water. Everything outside the SUV was vague and obscure, but from what he could tell, no one was around.

He peered into the gloom looking for an OPEN sign on one of the storefronts. He didn't see any.

This block had no bars or restaurants, so nothing was open.

He thought about where he was, and he remembered there was a gas station two blocks over. Hopefully, he could get a tow truck there.

But that meant walking in the rain for ten minutes. *Oh joy.*

Sergio leaned his head on the steering wheel. What a perfectly awful end to a perfectly awful week.

Sergio raised his head and looked at the still-wet stack of papers sitting on the passenger's seat. He had the urge to pick them up and throw them out in the rain. He could see himself doing it in his mind's eye. And he could see himself dancing around on top of them.

Blowing out air, Sergio motioned at his dead car and said, "Camel's back, meet your last straw."

The rain started coming down harder.

Sergio leaned back in his seat and closed his eyes. How had he gotten here?

After all his hard work. All his striving. All his determination. After all that, comes this? A broken-down

SUV in the middle of the night in the pouring rain?

Fine.

Sergio opened the door and stepped out into the weather. He was soaked immediately.

He slammed the SUV's driver's door, stomped forward two feet, and kicked the front tire as hard as he could.

"Ouch!" Sergio screamed. He hopped around on one foot and marveled at how much pain a toe could generate. Water slid down inside his collar, and his hopping foot splashed water up his pants leg.

Resisting the urge to kick his vehicle again, Sergio stomped away from it. Then he pulled his ruined suit jacket up over his head as a makeshift hood, and he sloshed over to the sidewalk. There, he put his head down and trudged away.

The streetlights provided enough illumination for him to see the sidewalk cracks and the curb. This was all he needed for navigation.

He'd gone just a block when the rain started to let up. Not really caring at that point because he was already wet through and through, Sergio kept walking. But then two things happened at once: The rain stopped entirely, and Sergio nearly tripped over an overstuffed green garbage bag lying in the middle of the sidewalk.

Sergio lowered his suit coat, and he looked around. The nearest streetlight poured pale yellow light down on a dumpster that had tipped partway over. Its contents were spilled all over the sidewalk.

Partially eaten food, sodden papers, and collapsed latte

cups were strewn all around. Sergio began taking careful steps through the trash.

He'd gone a couple of feet when the streetlight's glow hit something brightly colored. Sergio assumed it was a plastic bowl or cup, but even so, he glanced at it as he passed.

He stopped.

It wasn't a plastic bowl or cup.

It was . . . what was it?

Curious about the unique shape standing out among the ordinary refuse, Sergio took a step closer to it. It was a bright red propeller on top of a cap.

Leaning over, Sergio discovered that the propeller cap was attached to the round head of a small, maybe ten-inch-high, plastic figurine. The figurine was that of a small boy with reddish brown hair, big blue eyes, an orange triangular nose, rosy cheeks, and a wide mouth full of pronounced white teeth. The figurine's round head was matched in shape and size with the trunk of its body, which resembled a colorful bowling ball with arms and legs.

The figurine was wearing a short-sleeved, two-button shirt that had vertical red and blue stripes, matching the pattern on the cap. The shirt was tucked into solid blue pants, and the pants cuffs ended at the top of a pair of plain brown shoes. The shoes were more rounded than foot-shaped, but they matched the boy's fingerless, stumpy hands.

Both hands were occupied. The figurine's right

hand held a large red-and-yellow-striped balloon, and the figurine's right hand held a small sign that read I'M A LUCKY BOY.

"You are, are you?" Sergio playfully asked the figurine. "Do you have any tips? I could use some luck."

"I'm a lucky boy," the figurine said in a high-pitched child's voice.

Sergio widened his eyes and stared. This wasn't just a figurine. It was an electronic toy. Surprised the toy was still working despite sitting in the rain, he was intrigued enough to pick it up.

Wet, cold, hard, and slippery, the toy was light in weight. And though it looked old-fashioned, it was in great condition. No paint was scarred or faded.

Sergio turned the toy this way and that, looking for a control switch. He couldn't see one. He checked for a speaker and saw none. He even scanned for a battery compartment, but found nada.

Interesting. So was "I'm a lucky boy" all the toy said? Just for fun, Sergio decided to talk to the toy. "You say you're a lucky boy, like your sign says. Good for you."

"Good for you!" the toy said.

Oh, okay. The toy probably had some stock phrases to play and it was programmed to repeat back what it "heard," that is, recorded. Its inner workings were surprisingly well hidden; it didn't seem like a cheap toy.

Sergio decided to test his theory about the recording. He said, "Testing, testing."

The little toy didn't repeat the words. Instead, it said,

"It's lucky to be lucky!" Then it emitted a funny little *ha he he ha* giggle.

Sergio smiled. The giggle was infectious.

Sergio looked around. He was still alone. He looked back at the toy and shrugged.

"Do you have a name?" Sergio asked the toy.

"My name is Lucky Boy," the toy said.

Sergio snorted. "I never would have guessed."

Sergio wondered if Lucky Boy was worth anything. Probably not. But either way, he found he couldn't leave it lying there. It was unique, and it looked antique. He loved unique antiques. He'd make them part of his home decor.

Tucking the toy under his arm, Sergio walked on, and within five minutes, he was in the gas station convenience store making arrangements to have his car towed. While he signed paperwork, he set Lucky Boy on the counter.

The teenage clerk behind the counter called the tow-truck driver and then returned to the counter to watch Sergio sign papers. The teen was acne-spotted and limp-haired, but he was dressed in a clean blue uniform shirt with khaki pants, and he was friendly enough. "Sorry your car broke down, dude," he said. "Hey, do you want to buy a lottery ticket for tomorrow's drawing? It could help pay for car repairs."

"No thanks," Sergio said.

He was trying not to breathe deeply because the gas station convenience store smelled like pork rinds and dirty socks. But he involuntarily sucked in air when

Lucky Boy said, in his soprano-toned child's voice, "It's your lucky day!"

"Hey, dude," the teen said, "cool doll."

"It's not a doll."

"Okay. Whatever. It's still cool."

Sergio looked at Lucky Boy and shrugged. "Okay. I'll take that ticket after all. Who knows?"

"Exactly," the clerk beamed. He rang up a ticket.

It was nearly 3:00 a.m. when the tow-truck driver dropped Sergio off at his apartment building. Sergio didn't bother to explain Lucky Boy to the heavyset driver, who eyed the toy—and Sergio—with suspicion.

Tiptoeing through the hallway outside his apartment, he managed to open and close his door without being pestered. It seemed there *was* an hour past which Mrs. Bailey would not stay up. He looked at the toy he still carried. "Maybe it is my lucky day, after all."

Lucky Boy emitted his mischievous giggle.

Smiling, Sergio took Lucky Boy into his bedroom and set him on top of his cherry bureau next to the ceramic tray. Then he emptied his soggy pockets, stripped off his ruined clothes, took a hot shower, and fell into bed. Two and a half hours later, his alarm nearly catapulted him across the room.

Groaning, Sergio sleepwalked through getting dressed. Then he called a cab.

"Any wise words?" Sergio asked Lucky Boy before he left the apartment.

Lucky Boy giggled and said again, "Today's your lucky day."

Sergio couldn't say he agreed with that assessment, but technically, the day was still ongoing. Who knew what could happen? Running on just two and a half hours of sleep, he sure could use a little luck.

The day went by in a sleep-deprived blur. He was a walking zombie, and when Dale corrected him on his math for the tenth time, the last time being when Sergio added six and seven and came up with fifteen, he finally admitted, "Dale, I'm sorry. I'm asleep on my feet. My SUV broke down in the rain last night. I got two and a half hours of sleep."

"Go home," Dale said.

Sergio flinched. Was he being fired?

Dale laughed. "You're not being punished. We're not total ogres here. When you need sleep, you need sleep. Go home and sleep. When you come back, maybe you can tell me again what six plus seven is."

When Sergio let Violet know he was leaving, she offered to lend him her car. "I can get someone to take me to your place later to get it. Then we can go out to that gallery opening I wanted us to go to. You'll be rested up enough by the end of the day, right?"

Sergio started to nod. Then he stopped himself. He didn't want to go to a gallery opening. If this was his lucky day, didn't he deserve to tell the truth for a change?

He shook his head and refused to accept the car keys Violet was thrusting in his direction. "I'm just going to call a cab," he said. "Then I'm going to go to bed and sleep straight through until morning. I don't want to go out later."

Violet gave him the little pout he used to think was kind of cute. He turned away from her and headed back to his office to call a cab.

On his way home in the cab, Sergio heard a news report about "the big lottery," something about one of the winners buying a winning ticket at a gas station downtown. He wondered if it was the gas station he went to the previous night. He should check his ticket.

By the time Sergio returned home, though, he was in a semiconscious state. He didn't have enough energy to check his lottery ticket. Instead, he fell into bed and slept for four hours. He woke a little after 8:00 p.m. And feeling not even a little guilty about his latest lie to Violet, he ordered a pepperoni pizza. Taking it into his bed because he was still too tired to think, Sergio turned on the TV. The local news was ending.

The perky female coanchor said, "And to end on a light note, five people drew the winning numbers for the latest big jackpot. One of these tickets was bought right here in our town! Congratulations to the winner, whoever you are!"

That's right. The ticket.

Sergio jumped off the bed. He dashed to his ceramic tray and dug for the ticket. Grabbing it, he picked up his phone. Bringing up the winning numbers on the screen, he compared them to the numbers on his ticket.

He blinked and compared them again.

They matched! Every number matched!

Sergio jumped up and shouted, "Yes!"

Above him, Thunder Feet pounded on the floor.

"Same to you!" he shouted.

Sergio ran to the bureau and picked up Lucky Boy. He held the toy out like a dance partner and spun around the room. "You're brilliant. Absolutely brilliant!"

Lucky Boy sounded off his funny little giggle.

Sergio mimicked the giggle and threw himself on his bed. He kicked his feet in the air and whooped. Thunder Feet pounded again.

"To hell with you!" he shouted.

He wasn't going to put up with crap anymore. He had the means to fix all the problems he had in his life now.

Oh yeah. Things were going to change!

The next day, Sergio called in sick to work. When Violet telephoned later to check on him, he let the answering machine pick it up. Then he visited the lottery headquarters to claim his winnings. Because he was one of five people who had the winning numbers, after taxes, he ended up with just a little over $600,000. That was okay. It was plenty.

Back at home, Sergio relaxed in his living room and pondered what to do next. He had so many choices now!

The car repair place had called to tell him he'd had an oil leak that bled the vehicle dry of oil. The resulting engine damage would cost thousands to repair. Should he spend it or just sell the thing as it was for parts and get something new?

Grinning, Sergio stood and went to get Lucky Boy. Carrying the toy back into the living room, and feeling only a little silly, he asked Lucky Boy, "Should I repair my car or get a new one?"

"You deserve good things!" Lucky Boy sang out.

"You're right. I do." Sergio sat back and put Lucky Boy in his lap. "What kind of car do I deserve?"

"You deserve to have your dreams come true!"

"Really?"

Sergio thought about his dream car, the car he'd always wanted, a car that his father had once called "an impractical waste of money"—this from a man who had seventeen cars. Wasn't having more than two or three cars an impractical waste of money?

"You don't buy cars for flash, son," Tony always said. "You buy them for value. You buy flash and you're just asking to be ripped off. You'll pay more than the car is worth, and you'll be a magnet for car thieves."

"What if I like flash?" Sergio asked out loud now.

"You deserve flash!" Lucky Boy piped up.

"What should I buy?" Sergio asked.

"Buy a flashy sports car, the more expensive the better!"

Sergio fired off a finger gun at the little toy. "I like how you think."

He ignored the part of him that was a smidgeon creeped out by the fact that he was having a conversation with a toy. Lucky Boy had given him better advice than he'd ever gotten from anyone else. Who was he to care about where that advice came from?

So, he bought a bright red, expensive flashy sports car. High-end, highly visible, and as impressive as all get-out, Sergio's new car made him feel way more impressive than his silly aviator-style watch. And speaking of his watch . . .

"What kind of watch should I buy?" he asked Lucky Boy after he got home with his new car.

"You deserve bling!"

Sergio got dressed, and headed back out in his flashy car. He went to the best jewelry store in town, and he spent $37,000 on a new gold watch. It was impressive.

After he got the watch, he stopped and called Violet. She'd just gotten home from work.

"How would you like to have dinner at the Horizon?" he asked, grinning when she sucked in her breath. The Horizon was the best restaurant in town.

Violet squealed. "What's the occasion?"

"I'll tell you when I pick you up. Meet me out front of your building."

"I thought your SUV was still in the shop," she said.

"It is. I bought myself a new ride. It's red. You can't miss it."

"Okaaay," Violet said, drawing out the word as if she thought he'd lost his marbles.

He laughed and hung up, driving to Violet's apartment building and revving the engine as he neared her building. He stomped on the accelerator to zoom forward, then slammed on the breaks, coming to a screeching stop next to the curb just a foot from her. She stared in openmouthed shock at his new wheels.

"What do you think?" he asked as the powerful engine rumbled and she gaped at the car.

"How?" Violet asked. "Project managers don't make *that* much more than senior architects."

"Get in. I'll tell you about it."

Violet beamed at him as she opened the door.

Over a steak-and-lobster dinner, complete with huge slices of the most decadent chocolate cake he'd ever eaten, Sergio told Violet about his lottery win. He didn't, however, tell her about Lucky Boy. That somehow seemed like a secret he needed to keep to himself.

And he should have kept the lottery win to himself, too. Violet immediately started telling him how he should spend the money. "You should buy a boat," she told him as she plowed through her slice of cake. "We could go out on the lake every weekend. Oh, and you should buy a timeshare. Then we could go to different places every weekend. Or maybe we should just take a trip around the world. Oh, wait. A cruise. We should take a cruise. Or we could go . . ."

Sergio wasn't really listening to her. He was savoring the amazing chocolate cake. But he said "Mm-hm" at appropriate intervals . . . until he noticed she wasn't talking anymore. He also noticed when she whacked his knuckles with her fork.

"Ow! What?"

"I said, 'What is that?'" She gestured at his new watch.

"Oh, yeah." Sergio suddenly remembered. "I forgot to show this to you. I just got it this afternoon. It cost thirty-seven thousand dollars, but I deserve it." Sergio took another bite of cake.

Violet touched the watch reverently and beamed. She looked at him, her eyes bright. "So what did you get me? I was wondering all evening. I figured you had to have gotten me something since you won all that money. I figure you're saving it for the end of dinner. But now I can't wait any longer. What did you get me?"

Sergio set down his fork. He looked down.

"What?" Violet asked. "You did get me something, right?"

Sergio winced. "Um . . ."

"You got yourself a new sports car and a thirty-seven thousand dollars watch and you didn't get me *anything*?" Violet's voice rose at least an octave at the end of the question.

"I, uh . . ."

Think, he told himself. Surely, he could come up with some good reason he didn't buy her anything.

Violet stood and threw down her napkin. "Take me home right now."

Sergio didn't argue. He didn't have the energy. And, he realized, he didn't care that she was angry. He just took her home.

There, Violet got out of the car and started to walk away. Then she turned back and said, "You'd better have something for me tomorrow." She marched off, her hips swaying emphatically in her wake.

Sergio didn't give Violet a thought after he left her apartment building. He was feeling too good to be bothered by her tantrum.

When he got home, Sergio showed his watch to Lucky Boy. "What do you think?" he asked.

Lucky Boy giggled. "You look impressive!"

The next day, Sergio put on his new watch and went to work in his new car.

"Nice wheels," Clive said when he walked into Sergio's office a little after nine. "This position must pay more than I thought it did."

"Close the door," Sergio said.

He'd learned his lesson from Violet. Telling people about his lottery win could be tricky.

Clive raised his eyebrows and closed the door. He flopped into one of Sergio's visitor chairs. "What's the big secret? Did you rob a bank?"

"No!" Sergio grinned. He lowered his voice. "I won the lottery."

Clive laughed. "Good one."

"Really. I bought a ticket because—" Sergio stopped himself. He'd been about to tell Clive about Lucky Boy. He again got the strong feeling he should keep that bit to himself. He covered his near mistake by saying, "Because I had a whim. And I won."

Clive shook his head. "Good for you!" He spotted Sergio's watch. "Nice bling."

Sergio flushed. "I deserve some bling."

"Sure you do. So, what's next? Oh, I know. How about you buy your good friend Clive a swimming pool?"

Unlike Violet, Clive was kidding. Or at least Sergio hoped he was. He decided to go with a kidding response.

"Ha!" Sergio rolled his eyes. "Win your own lottery. Then you can buy your own swimming pool."

"Party pooper."

"When I buy my swimming pool, you can come and use it."

"Are you buying one?"

Sergio shrugged. "Actually, I'm not sure what I'm going to do next. I need to ask—"

Oops, he almost let it slip again.

Clive looked at him. "Who are you going to ask? Your mommy?"

Sergio flipped a pen at Clive. "Funny. No, not my mommy. I mean just ask, you know, in general. Like ask my intuition. Ask the universe. Like that."

"When did you get spiritual?"

"Having money is an exalting experience."

Clive laughed. "Well, even so, you'd better get to work. Dale was on a rampage yesterday about having to pick up your load because you were out sick. And the Jenkins project is kind of a mess."

Sergio frowned.

"I'm not criticizing," Clive said. "I couldn't do what you've been doing half as well as you have, but I'm just warning you that the powers that be aren't going to care about your car or your bling."

Sergio sighed. "You're right, obviously. I made a mess of things a couple days ago. I need to fix it."

Clive stood, leaned over Sergio's desk and raised his hand. "High five."

Sergio slapped Clive's hand.

"I'm honestly happy for you," Clive said. "Enjoy. Just don't cut off your nose to spite your face."

"What does that even mean?" Sergio asked.

"I'm not really sure. It's just what my mother said whenever I did something dumb in reaction to something. Actually, I don't think it's applicable here. But whatever. Just be careful with your decisions."

"Yes, Dad."

Clive laughed and left Sergio's office.

Sergio stared at his watch for several minutes and then got to work. And he was still working long after everyone else left . . . even Violet. She wasn't speaking to him. It was after midnight when he left the building and headed for his—

Where was his car?

His nice new bright and shiny sports car wasn't in his parking space.

What the heck?

Sergio turned a full circle in his empty parking spot. Then he sighed, went back inside his office, and called the police.

The police officer who took his stolen car report was nice enough to give Sergio a ride home. That was kind of fun. Sergio enjoyed listening to the chatter on the police radio, and he liked the way the leather creaked when he moved in his seat. He wasn't as keen on the weird smell coming from the back seat—a combination of bleach and something sour-smelling. He didn't ask about it.

"Sorry you got your car stolen the first full day you owned it," the young officer said when he pulled up outside Sergio's building. His name tag read, NEAL, which Sergio assumed was a last name. "That bites the big one."

Sergio unbuckled his seat belt and turned toward Officer Neal. He noticed the officer's buzz cut was recent; he could see white skin between his brown hair and the tan line on his neck.

"And you don't think I'll get it back?"

"It's probably out of the state by now," Neal said. "Or it's in parts." His voice broke often, like a teenager going through puberty.

Sergio shook his head. "Well, at least it was insured." He reached for the passenger door handle.

"Yeah, but they get you there, too. You'll get blue book for it, but that won't be as much as you paid for it. You're out taxes and license and all that."

Sergio smiled at Neal as he pushed the door open. "Well, you're a ray of sunshine,"

Neal laughed. "Sorry. This job tends to create pessimists."

Sergio marveled that Officer Neal had been on the job

long enough to become a pessimist. He wondered what Officer Neal's goals were. Did he have a big dream?

"Thanks for the ride," Sergio said as he got out of the squad car. He waved as Neal drove away, and he went in the front entrance of his building, whistling. He wasn't going to let this get him down. It was just a little setback. His luck had changed.

Or maybe not.

As he got in the elevator and pushed the button for the fourth floor, his upstairs neighbor dashed up behind him and shoved her way past him. He flicked a look of annoyance at her. She mistook it for something else.

"What are you looking at?" Thunder Feet snapped as she pounded on the fifth-floor button.

Wearing tight exercise pants and a sports bra, she must have thought he was admiring her. He wasn't. Not that she was bad-looking. She was actually cute—slender and just curvy enough, with blonde hair and a nice face. But she was too tall for him; she was at least five feet ten to his five feet seven. Not to mention her personality ruined everything about her looks.

"Nothing," Sergio said as the elevator made a clunking sound and started to rise. "Nothing at all."

Thunder Feet didn't smell good. She smelled like sweat and cigarette smoke. He concentrated on breathing through his mouth.

She sniffed and looked at him sideways. "You'd better not wake me up again tonight."

Sergio glanced at her incredulously. "Me, wake *you* up."

She glared at him. He ignored her as the elevator doors opened, and he got out on his floor.

One of the cheap beige carpet squares that covered the hallways in the building was sticking up just outside the elevator, and he tripped over it. He managed to catch himself, but he staggered a few feet before he did.

He heard her mutter, "Loser," as the elevator doors closed behind him. His shoulders tightened as he started down the hall, and by the time he was at his door, his good mood was slipping away.

And, just as he took out his keys, Mrs. Bailey threw her door open behind him and sang out, "I just made oatmeal-raisin cookies!"

Sergio whirled around and yelled, "I hate raisins!"

Mrs. Bailey, a plastic wrap–covered plate of cookies extended out in front of her, drew back. Her face bunched up in the middle like someone pulled on a drawstring attached to her skin.

Her lower lip quivered. "Well, why have you never said so?"

"I was being polite!" Sergio shouted. "But I don't feel like being polite right now. In fact, I don't feel like being *here* right now. I just want to be left alone."

Mrs. Bailey's eyes moistened. She nodded her head and quietly retreated into her apartment.

Sergio felt like a jerk, but he also felt exhilarated. Saying what he wanted was very freeing.

Inside his apartment, Sergio went through his usual post-work routine. When he finished, now wearing his sweats and T-shirt, he looked at Lucky Boy, who still sat, all jaunty and bright, on top of the bureau.

"So, what should I do now?" Sergio asked the toy.

"Everyone who's someone should have a house," Lucky Boy said.

Sergio stared at the toy's wide smile, and he began smiling just as wide. What a great idea! His own house!

Why not buy his own house? He had plenty of money now for a down payment. He said so to Lucky Boy, praising him with "You're brilliant."

Lucky Boy wasn't done throwing out ideas.

"Cash is king!" Lucky Boy said. "Go from bad to good!"

"That's even more brilliant!" This was the toy's best idea yet. He could buy an inexpensive fixer-upper with cash, gut it, and then completely redesign it. He could use all the skills he'd honed at the firm to create a true masterpiece of reinvention.

"You are so smart!" Sergio told Lucky Boy. He gave the toy a pat on one of his rosy cheeks.

Lucky Boy giggled.

Sergio headed to the phone. He needed to contact a real estate agent.

"To go places, you gotta have wheels," Lucky Boy said.

Sergio stopped. He turned to Lucky Boy and laughed. "Well, I'm glad someone in this room is thinking. I forgot I have no car." He frowned. "What should I get this time? The same thing?"

"You should have bigger and better," Lucky Boy said.

Sergio punched the air. "Perfect! You're absolutely right.

I'll get a big pickup!" He turned to head toward the phone again. "That's what I'll do first."

And he did.

In the morning, he drove his new, black, eight-cylinder, extra-cab, long-bed, lifted pickup with massive tires to work. Yeah, it was a Saturday, and he wished he could be out looking at houses, but since he'd missed work on Thursday he was totally behind. Even without missing that day, he'd have had to work today. Now he was going to have to work tomorrow, too.

When he parked it in his spot, he decided it looked even more impressive than the red sports car. Seeing the shiny black-and-chrome road monster sitting in his reserved spot almost made up for being at the office on Saturday for the third week in a row.

Sergio locked his truck and gave the hood a pat. He'd had the dealer add an upgraded security system to his new truck so he knew he'd find the truck here waiting for him at the end of the day. If someone tried to take this baby, that someone was going to have a very bad day.

The dealer had been happy to sell Sergio the security upgrade, but he'd been strangely against Sergio's request to have a full suspension lift added to the truck. Sergio would have thought the guy would be happy to make more money. But instead, he warned, "A lifted truck is a tilt or tip hazard. You'd be amazed at how easy it is to roll a truck when it's lifted."

Sergio thanked him for the warning, but told him to do it anyway. And he was glad he did.

Sergio strutted into the office feeling like he was at least three inches taller than he was before. He felt even taller when he got to his office and received a phone call from his insurer. They were going to pay out the full purchase price of his stolen vehicle, and the taxes and licensing costs were being refunded because they didn't go through before the car was taken. So much for Officer Neal's pessimism. *Ha!* Sergio was on a roll!

Or maybe not.

When Sergio got off the phone, he looked up to find Violet standing in his office doorway. Because it was Saturday, she was dressed casually. She wore tight jeans with a flouncy hem and a filmy yellow blouse with a feathered fringe. As she tapped her foot, the flouncy hem bounced, and her fringe danced.

"I knew I'd find you here," Violet said.

"Oh, hi, Violet."

"Don't 'Oh, hi, Violet' me."

Sergio frowned. He really needed to get back to work. "What's wrong?"

"What's wrong?" Violet uncrossed her arms and stomped to his desk. She recrossed her arms and looked down at him. "Did you buy me a present yet?"

Sergio pressed his lips together. Oops. He hadn't even thought of it.

"I've been really busy," Sergio said.

Violet snorted. "You're not really going to try that, are you? With that ridiculous truck sitting outside? It had to take time to buy that monstrosity. You could manage the time to go to the dealership and you couldn't pop into a jewelry store and get me a little something?"

"I'm sorry, Violet. I have no excuse. I've just been so wrapped up in the excitement of it all."

"Wrapped up in yourself, you mean."

"Is that so bad?"

"What? Being selfish? Yeah, that's bad."

Sergio glared at her. "If it's selfish to be wrapped up in yourself, then you're kind of the pot calling the kettle black, aren't you?"

"What? What kind of insult is that?"

"You've never heard the idiom, the pot calling the kettle black?"

"Sure, but . . ." She raised her eyebrows. "Are you calling me selfish?"

"If the shoe fits."

"Well, screw you and your stupid idioms."

Before Sergio could say anything else, Violet stormed out of his office. For several seconds, Sergio stared after her. Then he shrugged and went back to work.

At the end of a very long day, Sergio dragged his tired body to his impressive new truck. He was frustrated: Even if he returned tomorrow and worked all day, he'd still be way behind on Monday morning. At this rate, he was never going to be able to look for a house, much less have time to renovate one.

He knew he wasn't home enough these days to really worry about what his home looked like, but he was tired of living under Thunder Feet and tired of living across the hall from Mrs. Bailey. Besides, he deserved to live someplace better than this cubic apartment building with its cheap carpet squares.

But how could he move *and* work? There weren't enough hours in the day.

And what was he going to do about Violet?

As soon as he changed clothes, Sergio asked Lucky Boy this very question.

"You deserve to be happy," Lucky Boy said.

"I agree," Sergio said. "But . . ." He sat down on the edge of his bed. "Violet doesn't make me happy."

This was a little bit of a revelation. "Huh," Sergio said.

He thought back over his year with Violet. Had she *ever* made him happy?

Not exactly. Not really. No, not at all.

Having a girlfriend made him feel good. He'd never had one in high school or college. All he'd done was pine for the out-of-reach Sophia in high school, and in college, he never had time for dating. He'd gone out a few times since then, but Violet was his first steady girl. And that's why he dated her: not because she made him happy, but because she kept going out with him. Having a steady girl-friend made him feel impressive.

"What should I do about Violet?" Sergio asked Lucky Boy again.

"If it's broken, fix it or get rid of it," Lucky Boy said.

That seemed like good advice.

Did Sergio want to fix things with Violet?

No, he did not.

Okay. Then the solution was simple. He leaned over to his nightstand and picked up the phone. He dialed Violet.

When she picked up, it was obvious she'd been sleeping. "H'lo," she breathed into the phone.

"Violet, I—"

"What time is it, Sergio? Can't you wait until a reasonable time to call and apologize?"

Sergio rolled his eyes. "I'm not calling to apologize. I'm calling to break up with you."

"What? It sounded like you just said—"

"Break up with you. That is what I said. I don't want to go out with you anymore."

Violet was silent. But she was still on the phone. He could hear her breathing.

"I should have realized it when I didn't buy you anything. If I loved you and really wanted to be with you, buying you something should have been a no-brainer. But I—"

"Forget you, Sergio," Violet said. "You're not good enough for me anyway. You're a funny-looking little man, and I'm too much of a catch for you." Violet slammed down her phone, and the line went dead.

Sergio sat for a second to see if he felt bad. He didn't.

He looked at Lucky Boy. "Great advice."

Lucky Boy giggled.

Okay, so Sergio's girlfriend problem was solved. But what about his job? How could he be happy and work the kind of hours he was working?

"What should I do about my job?" Sergio asked Lucky Boy.

"Better things are on the horizon."

Sergio sank down onto his bed. Wow. He'd never thought . . .

He stared at Lucky Boy, and Lucky Boy's big blue eyes stared back. Why hadn't Sergio thought of that?

Why was he still at his job?

He hadn't been happy at the firm for some time, and instead of looking for something else, he'd just applied for the project manager job. Talk about thinking inside the box.

He had to get out of the box! *Way* out of the box.

Sergio stood and started pacing back and forth by his bed. The seed of an idea was sprouting in his mind. What if . . . ?

He turned and looked at Lucky Boy. "What do you think of me starting my own business?"

"You deserve to be your own boss," Lucky Boy said. "It would be impressive!"

Sergio grinned. Yes, it would.

He thought about his dad.

Even though Tony never said so, he was disappointed in his son's career. Sergio felt it every time Tony asked his stupid skyscraper question.

"This country runs on the backbone of entrepreneurialism," Tony liked to say. "Men like me keep our nation strong."

If Sergio wanted to make his dad proud, he needed to be an entrepreneur. And he knew just how to do it.

But first, he had to quit his job.

Which he did the next morning.

"You're really quitting?" Clive said when he walked into Sergio's office fifteen minutes after Sergio informed Dale he was done with the new job.

"What the hell are you playing at?" Dale had asked. The top of his bald head turned red as he yelled, "You apply for a pivotal job, get it, make hash of it, and then you quit? You realize you're *done* at this firm, too, right?"

Sergio nodded. "Well, yes. That was going to be the next thing I told you. I'm quitting entirely."

"What the hell is wrong with you?" Dale shouted. "You're our brightest architect! You're throwing your career away."

Sergio shrugged. "You can think that if you want. I'm going to go into business for myself."

Dale guffawed. "Oh, that's rich. You'll be homeless in no time."

Sergio shrugged again. "Nope. I'm going to be a success-ful, impressive entrepreneur."

Dale shook his head and strode out of Sergio's office.

"Yes," Sergio said to Clive now. "I'm really quitting."

Clive leaned against the wall and watched Sergio put his personal belongings in a cardboard box. "What are you going to do?"

"Get outside the box."

Clive laughed and pointed at Sergio's arms, which were both currently *inside* the box on his desk. Sergio smiled, too.

"You know what I mean."

"Not exactly, but I wish you luck."

"Oh, I have a lot of luck now. I have Lucky Boy." He laughed, and he noticed his laugh sounded, oddly, a little like Lucky Boy's giggle.

Oops. He hadn't meant to say that.

Clive frowned. "You're a lucky boy? Is that what you just said?"

Sergio blinked and lied. "Sure."

Clive held out a fist, and Sergio bumped it with his.

"Keep in touch," Clive said.

"I will," Sergio said.

But he didn't.

He had too much going on.

For one thing, he had to find the right place to renovate into a new home.

Sergio thought finding a fixer-upper was going to be easy. The town was full of them, and after years of working on residential renovations, he knew plenty of real estate agents. Which one should he call?

Sergio sat at his small retro dining room table and ate kung pao chicken out of the carton while he pondered his upcoming house hunt. Lucky Boy sat on the table in front of him.

It occurred to Sergio as he ordered his dinner that leaving the toy in the bedroom was a little discourteous. After all, Lucky Boy had been the catalyst for a lot of great things in Sergio's life, and that was only in a few days. Here Sergio was, a man of leisure who was about to embark on an impressive entrepreneurial adventure, and he was rudely ignoring the little guy who had made it all possible. And so, he brought Lucky Boy out to join him for dinner.

"I wish I could share this with you," Sergio said to Lucky Boy. "But I don't think toys eat."

Sergio forked up some of the spicy chicken. He chewed, swallowed, and mused, "So, which real estate agent should I pick?"

"Pretty is good," Lucky Boy said.

Sergio looked at Lucky Boy. "Well, aren't you a little Casanova? Didn't I just get rid of a girlfriend?"

Lucky Boy giggled.

"Are you saying I should find a better one?"

Lucky Boy giggled again.

"Okay," Sergio said. "Pretty. Let's see." He thought about the agents he knew.

One of them, Eve, was very pretty. But he was also reasonably sure she was married.

"Pretty doesn't do us any good if she's married," he pointed out.

"You deserve a great girl who dotes on you."

"Yes, I do."

Violet had never doted on him. Good riddance to her. Someone better was out there. He thought for a minute.

He snapped his fingers. There was an agent named Claire Fredericks who was petite and soft-spoken. They once had a conversation about science fiction, and she said she liked it. That was a good start, wasn't it? As far as Sergio knew, she was single.

He picked up the phone and called Claire to schedule an appointment to look at houses the next day.

Sergio's father would like Claire, Sergio decided as he sat with her at a conference table in her real estate office. Not only was Claire small and slender, but she was dark-haired, too. She looked Italian. He didn't know if she was, but she looked it. That would be good enough for Tony.

And he could hear his mother now. "Oh, the babies you could make together." She always said that when she tried to set him up with an Italian girl.

"What exactly did you have in mind?" Claire asked, swiveling to face Sergio.

Sergio decided that Claire wasn't what most people would call "pretty." Her features were a little too strong for that. But he thought she was eye-catching. She had huge, somewhat almond-shaped, very dark brown eyes. He thought of them as comic book eyes. Claire's face would make a great superhero face.

This close to her, he could smell her perfume, which was light but distinctive. It smelled like a combination of fruit and flowers, kind of citrusy and kind of sweet. He liked it. He had to force himself to think about houses instead of about Claire.

"I recently came into a substantial amount of money," Serge told her, "and I want to leverage it into not just a new home for me but a multimillion-dollar design business. To that end, I want something that needs a total overhaul.

And I'm thinking something industrial maybe, something with massive architectural potential. Is there anything available in the old warehouse district, the part that was rezoned?"

Claire nodded several times. "Oh, how exciting. I'd love to be part of helping you build a multimillion-dollar business. And I think your plan is excellent. Your design aesthetic is perfect for that kind of building rehab."

"I didn't know you'd noticed my design aesthetic," Sergio said. He blushed.

Claire smiled at him. "I notice more than I let on."

Sergio smiled back at Claire. He was sure she was flirting with him.

Claire cleared her throat. "There are several properties that fit your description, but there's one in particular I think will be perfect for you. Do you want to go see it?"

"Absolutely."

They went to see it. And it *was* perfect.

The perfect property was an old stand-alone warehouse that was just at the edge of the area recently rezoned to residential. This meant it got the best of both worlds. It fit with the other warehouse rebuilds around it, but it also backed up to the lush greenery of the neighboring, well-established residential area.

At 5,500 square feet, the property was ideal for what Sergio wanted to do with it, which was to make a spacious living area with a lot of architectural wow and an adjoining office space with even more eye-catching structural features. The warehouse had a brick exterior that was in fantastic condition, and its interior support beams and load-bearing walls looked sound. Yes, it was an impressive building, and Sergio absolutely deserved it.

But it cost more than he'd planned to spend.

Sergio did some calculations. He'd already gotten the insurance payout on the car and the refund of the tax and license fees. The truck hadn't cost as much as the sports car, so he was ahead there. If he bought this old warehouse, he was pretty sure he'd have enough left to complete the renovations. Should he go for it?

Of course he should.

"Let's make an offer," Sergio said to Claire.

She clapped her hands, then got down to business writing up the offer.

"I'll go present this right now. I expect the owner to accept it."

"Do you want to go to dinner to celebrate when he does?" Sergio blurted.

Claire studied him for a moment. Then she did a cute little half shrug, and said, "Sure."

Sergio grinned. "I'm so glad I called you."

Claire smiled back. "Me too."

Sergio went home to wait for word on his offer. There, he told Lucky Boy what happened. Lucky Boy giggled.

While he waited for Claire's call telling him he got the place, Sergio started making sketches of his ideas for it. He'd already drawn plans for the whole first floor when Claire called.

"You got it!" she said when he answered.

"Great!"

"I need to wrap up a couple things, and then I'll be free for the evening."

"Can I pick you up?" Sergio asked.

"Sure."

They set a time, and Sergio hung up.

He looked at Lucky Boy. "Where should I take her to dinner?" he asked. "I want to impress her."

"You deserve to go where you want," Lucky Boy said. "Impress yourself."

Sergio laughed. "You're right. I should impress me for a change. Well, I like that Mexican place downtown, the one with the fountain in the courtyard. I'll take her there."

Lucky Boy giggled.

Sergio played with his plans for a few more minutes, and then he got ready for dinner, putting on a pair of casual black slacks and a gray-and-black-striped dress shirt. He grabbed a black leather jacket to finish off the ensemble, and he started toward the door, only cringing a little when Thunder Feet started a two-step on his ceiling. When he reached the door, his gaze fell on Lucky Boy, who still sat on the table.

Sergio felt bad leaving Lucky Boy home alone. He was giving Sergio all this great advice. Did he deserve to sit around like a knickknack in an empty apartment?

No way.

Sergio picked up Lucky Boy, tucked him under his arm, and headed out the door. When Sergio glanced at

Mrs. Bailey's closed door before he walked down the hall, Lucky Boy giggled.

Mrs. Bailey hadn't bothered Sergio since his raisin outburst. He was hoping her hurt feelings, or whatever was keeping her inside her own walls, would hold until he'd moved into his new place.

In his lifted truck, Sergio put Lucky Boy in one of the cupholders in the console. When that put Lucky Boy in more of a hole than seemed polite, Sergio dug some paperwork out of the glovebox, folded it up, and made a sort of elevated seat for Lucky Boy.

Lucky Boy giggled.

"You might not want to do that when Claire's around," Sergio said, starting the engine.

"Other people's judgments are irrelevant," Lucky Boy said.

Sergio glanced at his new friend. "You're right, actually. Okay, laugh if you want to."

Lucky Boy giggled.

Sergio pulled out of his parking garage. "Do you think I should take her something? Flowers? Too much or not enough?"

"Roses speak from the heart," Lucky Boy said.

"Okay. Roses it is."

Sergio stopped by a florist and bought a dozen pink roses. Judging from Claire's bright eyes and big smile when she spotted them on the dashboard, he made a good choice.

She looked from the flowers to Sergio. "For me?"

"Of course."

She reached out for them and then frowned.

"What's wrong? Are you allergic?"

"No. No, I was just thinking they'll wilt while we're at dinner."

Sergio shook his head. "I had them put those little vials of water on the end of each stem."

Claire looked at him and smiled widely. Then she hugged him. "You're so thoughtful!"

Sergio accepted the hug and gave Lucky Boy a thumbs-up behind Claire's back.

As soon as Claire was buckled into her seat, she noticed Lucky Boy. She picked him up.

"What's this?"

Sergio tensed, feeling strangely possessive of the little guy. "That's Lucky Boy. He's . . . sort of like a mascot."

Claire gave him a puzzled look.

Sergio hesitated, then decided to go ahead and tell her the whole story. Before, it had seemed wrong to talk about Lucky Boy, but now it felt disrespectful not to talk about him. Not telling the truth felt like Sergio was taking credit for the recent turn of events his life had taken. Lucky Boy should have some recognition.

Sergio told Claire the whole story.

Claire listened with rapt attention, her brows going higher and higher as the story went on. When Sergio was done, she turned Lucky Boy over. "How does it work?"

Sergio shrugged.

"You're not curious? You don't want to take it apart and find out?" She started tugging on Lucky Boy's arms.

Sergio grabbed Lucky Boy away from Claire. "No!"

Claire's eyebrows climbed a notch higher.

"Sorry," Sergio said. "I guess I'm sentimental about it."

Claire looked from Lucky Boy to Sergio and back. "I understand," she said.

Sergio didn't think she did. But he didn't say anything else, and by then, they'd arrived at the restaurant.

The next few weeks passed in a blur. While Sergio was waiting for the deal to close, he finished his designs. Then he submitted them for approval to the city permit offices while he talked to contractors. He was looking for exactly the right team to work on his project, and it didn't take him long to find it. Soon after that, he got approval, and the renovation began.

Also, Sergio moved in to his new place.

He wasn't planning on leaving his old apartment before the renovations to his new place were done, but his lease came up for renewal, and he'd get a penalty if he left before the end of the year. That made no sense, so he let the lease lapse.

He hired movers to pack up his stuff and move everything to the new property. So long, Thunder Feet. So long, Mrs. Bailey.

Although the warehouse was a mess—filled with piles of demolished wood, concrete and drywall, a maze of walls stripped to the studs, exposed pipes and wiring—Sergio was able to clear out a corner of it to stack his belongings, store his furniture, and set up his bed. He had electricity, and one working bathroom. But he had no kitchen. He bought a small fridge for things like milk and sandwich fixings, but mostly, he figured he could eat out or get take-out. It was basically urban camping.

Sergio felt like he did when he was a little kid starting a new adventure.

"What do you think?" he asked Lucky Boy when he set the toy on top of a pile of boxes near the bed. Sergio did his patented moonwalk and spin, and he threw his arms out and up. "Isn't this place going to be great?"

"You deserve the best," Lucky Boy said.

"This *will* be the best when it's done."

Lucky Boy giggled.

Sergio once again found himself having long days, but being his own boss, he didn't mind it so much. He was enjoying overseeing his project . . . until he wasn't. And he was enjoying Claire . . . until he wasn't.

The problem with the project was money. It turned out that he'd underestimated costs. He didn't have a budget big enough to do all he wanted to do. And if he couldn't do what he wanted to do, he wouldn't create an impressive space. If he didn't create an impressive space, he wouldn't be able to use his home as a platform for getting clients.

"Where can I get more money?" Sergio asked Lucky Boy one evening.

"Rich people have lots of money!"

Sergio wasn't sure what to make of that, but he figured Lucky Boy would make it clear soon enough. Lucky Boy always told him what to do.

By now, Sergio was taking Lucky Boy wherever he went. Lucky Boy helped him all day long. He helped Sergio pick out materials, make design decisions, and manage his time. He even helped Sergio choose his food. Lucky Boy also advised him on other purchases, like all the electronics he was buying for the new place and all the casual clothes he was buying to replace his more formal work wardrobe. When Sergio worried about going through his money, Lucky Boy said, "You deserve the best."

Lucky Boy had the same thing to say about Claire.

Everything with Claire was great at first. She appreciated the places he took her and the flowers and gifts he brought her. But when money got tighter, and he had to stop giving her gifts and start suggesting they stay home for takeout, she began changing. Oh, she still acted sweet and all, but he was sure he could sense an undertone in the things she said. "Of course, I don't mind having a picnic on the floor of your place," sounded like "Where do you get off making me sit on the floor, cheapskate?" It wasn't her words exactly; it was the *inflections* of her words.

And then there were the ways she was trying to improve him. She went about it in a sneaky way. She wouldn't tell him she didn't like his shirts, for example; she just bought him "gifts" of new shirts. She didn't tell him she hated his taste in music; she just bought him new CDs. It was becoming annoying.

And then there were the "helpful" suggestions. When he was complaining that he wished he was taller, she said, "Well, you could always have lifts put in your shoes, sweetie." Why couldn't she have been supportive and said, "Don't be silly, you're plenty tall!" He was getting tired of coming up short, literally and figuratively.

When Sergio asked Lucky Boy about Claire, he said, "You deserve the girl of your dreams!"

Sergio agreed. He needed to stop wasting his time with women who weren't right for him. There was only one girl for him, and that girl was Sophia. He couldn't have her in high school, but things were different now. Not only did he deserve to have her, but she would be lucky to have him!

He was going to have to break up with Claire.

Unfortunately, a meet-the-parents dinner was coming up. His mother had been bugging him to set it up for weeks, and the week before, she'd called, ostensibly to tell him he'd received his third invitation to his tenth high school reunion. But once she had him on the phone, she said, "When are we going to get to meet your Claire? You keep putting me off, Sergio. It's not nice to put your mother off. Three weeks ago, you said, 'Next week.' Two weeks ago, you said, 'Next week.' A week ago—"

"I get it, Mama."

"So?"

"So how about this week?" he said.

"Perfect," his mother said. "You'll come on Saturday."

Now he wished he hadn't agreed.

"Should I cancel the dinner?" he asked Lucky Boy.

"Your father is rich!" Lucky Boy said. "Go to dinner. Get a loan."

Sergio had never asked his dad for money, but Lucky Boy was right. Tony was rich. Why not ask for a loan when he went for the dinner?

He'd have to break up with Claire after that.

As Sergio suspected, his parents liked Claire on sight. His mother fussed over Claire so much, he said, "She's not royalty, Mama."

"Well, I'm just being friendly." His mother patted her graying black hair, which she had twisted into an elaborate bun. She smoothed the full skirt of her emerald-green cocktail dress. His mother liked to "get dolled up."

Claire lifted her chin and said, "Sergio, don't you know all women want to be treated like royalty?"

"Fine," Sergio said. "Then I'm going to leave you regal ladies here. I need to talk to Papa."

Tony had greeted Sergio and Claire and then retreated back into his study. His work wasn't done for the day. But he boomed, "Come in," when Sergio knocked on the door.

Sergio stepped into his father's domain. As always, he stopped and looked in awe at the space. Tony loved historic architectural details, and he'd designed an office filled with so many carved wood features and so many filigreed trimmings that it looked like something out of the sixteenth century. It was a massive office, over a thousand square feet, and it vaulted two stories. Lined with bookshelves stuffed with books, the room had a rolling ladder for the tall shelves and a spiral staircase to an upper balcony.

"She's a prize," Tony said to Sergio before motioning

Sergio onto a plush maroon leather couch by the brick fireplace.

"Hm," Sergio said.

Tony lowered himself into his recliner. "But you're not here to talk about her. What's on your mind, son?"

"I need a loan," Sergio said. He'd decided to be direct.

"I thought you won all that money."

"I've spent nearly all of it."

Tony's bushy white eyebrows rose.

"Papa, you always said you have to spend money to make money. And that's what I'm doing. I have to create a mind-blowing renovation, something so good that it's going to be featured in architectural and design magazines and even the newspaper. I need to create buzz; that's what will get me clients. If you could loan me just a couple hundred thousand, I can create what I want and then my business will be off and running. I'll pay you back really fast."

Tony ran a hand through his curly white hair. He smoothed his mustache then tapped the side of his long nose, the nose he'd unfortunately handed down to Sergio.

"Okay," Tony said. "I'll loan you the money. But it's a short-term loan. If you can't pay it back in six months, you'll pay it back in labor."

Sergio, who had been starting to smile, frowned. "What do you mean?"

"You'll have to come drive a truck for me."

Sergio stared at his father. Then he shrugged. Why not agree to it? He'd be able to pay back the loan before that would happen.

Still, the exchange concerned him.

Over dinner, his concerns turned into full-blown annoyance.

They had dinner al fresco, sitting at the iron-and-glass table on the stone patio in the back garden. It would have been a nice meal if Claire hadn't kept sniping at him. "Do you want to try some of my roasted brussels sprouts?" she asked him at one point. "They're really good."

Sergio's mother found the question amusing. "Sergio doesn't like brussels sprouts, Claire, dear. He's like his father; they just don't appreciate good vegetables."

Tony ignored the comment. Sergio couldn't. It bothered him. Where did Claire get off telling him what he should like?

In the car on the way home, Sergio did what he needed to do.

Claire was chattering about how lovely his parents' home was. "Have you ever thought about designing a big house like that?" she asked.

Sergio didn't bother to answer the question. He said, "I don't want to date you anymore,"

Claire looked at him. "What did you say?"

"You heard me. I don't want to date anymore. All you do is find fault with me. I don't like it."

"Find fault? How do I find fault?"

"The shirts. The CDs."

"What? Giving you gifts is finding fault?"

"You told me I should wear lifts."

"You said you felt short; I was just trying to be helpful!"

"You don't like my taste in vegetables."

"I was just telling you mine tasted good!"

"I don't know why you go out with me if there's so much wrong with me," Sergio complained.

Claire crossed her arms and glared at him. "You're being ridiculous!"

"Yeah? See? Now you think I'm ridiculous."

Claire sighed. "You've lost your mind."

Riding in the console as always these days, Lucky Boy giggled.

Claire picked up Lucky Boy and shook the toy in Sergio's direction. "And you play with dolls."

Sergio grabbed for Lucky Boy. "Put him down!" He turned to look at Claire, and the truck swerved.

Claire held Lucky Boy away from Sergio. "You've started treating it like a guru, and I was going along with it. But really, Sergio. It's a tchotchke, a doll, a little statue. It's not your personal guide through life. If you think it is, you're a weirdo." Claire pressed the button to lower her window. "You need to get rid of this thing." She raised her arm to toss Lucky Boy out of the truck.

Sergio lunged for Lucky Boy, and as he did, he wrenched the wheel.

They were heading into a curve, and the lifted truck couldn't handle the severe turn. It tipped right over, left the road, and headed down the rocky embankment. Suddenly, they were upside down. Then right side up. Then upside down. Every flip of the vehicle was accompanied by the screech and crunch of metal against rock. Every jolt threw them around within the confines of their seat belts, which jerked against their bodies.

Thankfully, Sergio was able to grab Lucky Boy away from Claire as the truck started going over, so the toy wasn't damaged. The truck landed right side up, but its roof was smashed down toward their heads.

Claire started screaming the second the truck stopped moving. Sergio worked as fast as he could to undo his seat belt and himself. He wanted to get out of the compressed space filled with Claire's hysterical shrieking. He managed to kick his crumpled door open and stumble out.

Just as he turned to help Claire, another truck stopped. "Are you okay?" a middle-aged man called out.

Sergio took stock. He'd gotten jostled about, for sure. It felt like he'd pulled a couple muscles, and he knew he'd have bruises, but nothing was broken. He looked at Claire. She didn't seem to have anything broken, either. He saw no blood. She looked like she was more angry than injured.

"We're okay," he called out.

"Speak for yourself," Claire snapped. "You're going to pay for this."

"I'll go get help," the middle-aged man shouted.

Sergio called out, "Thanks!"

The truck was a mess. After it was towed, Sergio found out it would need thousands of dollars in bodywork, and it would be in the shop for a couple weeks.

Suddenly, Sergio was without a vehicle again. He was also

without a girlfriend. And soon, he was facing a lawsuit. Claire was suing him for negligence resulting in her injuries.

Because Sergio couldn't get to suppliers to choose finishes for his renovation, work started slowing down. On top of that, unbeknownst to Sergio, his contractor had had a thing for Claire, and he quit after the accident. "I can't in good conscious work for a man who hurts women," the contractor said.

That set Sergio's project back a full month, but he wasn't worried. It would all come together.

Besides, it wasn't important. He had something far more exciting to think about.

The day after Sergio broke up with Claire, he had called his mother to ask if she could get him Sophia's phone number. Before he could ask, though, his mother told him he'd received yet another invitation to his high school reunion.

How lucky was that? It would be even better than calling her. He'd meet up with Sophia at the reunion and wow her and the rest of the class, too!

"Hey, Mama," he said, "you know Sophia Manchester's mama, right?"

"Sophia, that lovely girl from your class? Yes, we're good friends."

"Could you find out if she's going to the reunion?"

His mother let out a little squeal. "Oh, my Sergio is so clever. Yes, I can do that. That Claire was a nice girl, but Sophia is much better for you."

"I agree, Mama."

Content that the perfect girl was once more in his

sights, Sergio returned his attention to his renovations until he heard from his mother. It didn't take long for her to get back to him. When she called him, she was bubbling with enthusiasm.

She shouted in his ear, "Sergio, she's definitely coming. Sophia will be at the reunion!"

Sergio hung up the phone grinning from ear to ear. Not only was he getting the time he needed to catch up on the renovation, but he was also going to get the girl of his dreams.

The next two and a half weeks passed quickly. Sergio didn't make as much progress on the renovation as he wanted, but he wasn't concerned. He finally had his truck back, so things were going to go faster now.

"You have all the time you need," Lucky Boy told him.

He was, however, running out of time to get ready for his reunion.

"What should I do to get ready for the reunion?" Sergio asked Lucky Boy after he polished off a burger one evening. "I have the right clothes. But I think I should do more. I want to knock Sophia's socks off! I think I should go above and beyond. What do you think?"

Sergio was still living pretty much on his bed. The rest of his furniture was stacked up and covered with plastic to keep it free of the paint spatters and dust created by the renovations.

He leaned back on his pillow and looked at his little buddy, who now had his own pillow next to Sergio's on the bed.

"Be the best to get the best," Lucky Boy said.

Well, Sergio was the best architect, and he was going to have the best business.

"But what about my looks?" Sergio said. "I know I'm smart, but smart never counted for much in high school. When I go to the reunion, everyone's going to look at me and see just a ten-year-older version of who I was then. I want to go back looking different! And I have to admit, I do have some flaws in my appearance. My ears, for instance—they're too big. What should I do about my ears?"

"You don't need them," Lucky Boy said.

"What does that mean? I don't need my ears?" Sergio was confused.

"You're better off without them!"

"Do you think so? Really?" Sergio asked.

"Get rid of what you don't need."

Sergio nodded. "That makes sense."

He thought about going to the reunion without his big dopey ears sticking out. That would be so great!

But his ears weren't the only issue.

"I still won't look the way I want to, even without my big ears. I'd really like to look perfect for the reunion."

"You deserve perfection," Lucky Boy said.

"Exactly! You're right. I do."

Sergio leaned over to the box he used as a nightstand. He grabbed a pad of paper and a pen. "Okay, Lucky Boy, you need to help me here. Let's figure out what I can do to be the best me for the reunion. Let's make a list so I know exactly what I need to do."

"Make a plan for perfection!"

Sergio grinned. "That's just what I'm going to do!" He tapped the paper with the pen. "Okay, well, besides my ears," he said, "I hate my hair." He scribbled on the paper.

"Hair is overrated," Lucky Boy said.

Lucky Boy was right. Hair was a lot of work. Dale had a shaved head, and women found him attractive.

Sergio made a note, but then he frowned. He remembered Dale talking about how much work it was to maintain a perfectly shaved head—more work even than keeping hair nice. Shaving wasn't going to do it. His hair would grow back if he didn't go deep. He scratched out his previous note and wrote a new one.

He thought for a few seconds. "My eyes are too small. I look like a bird. I have beady eyes. What can I do about my eyes?"

"Eyelids cover eyes."

"Good point," Sergio said. He made another note. "My nose is too long."

"Cut to fit. That's the rule," Lucky Boy said.

Sergio nodded. *Of course!* When wood was too long, you trimmed off the end. He wrote on the pad.

"My lips are too thick," Sergio said. "They look like a girl's lips."

"Wood carvers are artists," Lucky Boy said.

"Another good point," Sergio said. Why hadn't he thought of that? He was a master at reshaping wood; he was sure he could reshape anything. He scribbled another note. Then he said, "I want to be taller."

"Remove and reuse," Lucky Boy said.

Sergio smiled. *Right!* He often took scrap material from one part of a project and repurposed it for another part. He made a note.

Then he wondered, "What should I do about my belly?"

"Leaner is meaner," Lucky Boy said. "Trim the fat."

Sergio nodded and wrote on his list.

He smiled warmly at Lucky Boy. "You're a great help. I'm so glad I found you."

Lucky Boy giggled.

Sergio sat and wrote for a bit longer, and then he stood. "Okay. Time to get to work."

Sergio crossed to his stacks of boxes, and moved them around until he found the one he wanted. Tearing off the tape, he reached in and pulled out his kitchen knife set. He put it on the bed. Setting the first box aside, he examined the surrounding boxes until he found the next one he wanted. He ripped the tape from that box and pulled out a pair of scissors, needles and thread, a measuring tape, and some twine. He laid all of these items out on the bed.

He stepped into the makeshift bathroom area and got his razor. He added that to what he'd already gathered.

Then he left his little carved-out living space and walked out into the unfinished great room. "I should have the rest of what I need out here." He looked around.

He spotted a box cutter on what was going to become the kitchen island, and he picked it up. Then he looked around again. His gaze landed on his drill. That would come in handy.

Now where had he put his wood-carving knives? He had a whole set of them. They were extra sharp, for exact contouring.

Ah, there they were. He found them tucked behind his router. Pondering it for a moment, he picked it up, too, and he grabbed the set of bits that went with it.

He surveyed the space again. He needed one more thing.

He saw what he was looking for on the far side of the room. He crossed over, picked up a handsaw, and returned to his living area.

He added his new tools to the collection on the bed. He looked at Lucky Boy.

"What do you think? Do I have everything?"

"The right tools for the right jobs!"

Sergio felt a rush of excitement. This was going to be awesome. He was finally going to fix himself up so he'd be as eye-catching as he was successful.

Sergio did a moonwalk along the foot of the bed. He spun in a circle and looked at his assembled tools.

Where to begin?

Sergio's class reunion was being held in the grand ballroom of the oldest hotel in town. He was excited about that because the ballroom was impressive. With gilded, ornate ceilings and carved panel walls, filled with crystal chandeliers and fine artwork, the room was exactly the kind of room that would make a great backdrop for Sergio's new and impressive look.

He was going to drop some jaws this evening. That was

for sure. He decided to arrive late so he had the biggest audience possible for his grand entrance.

Thankful to have his big truck to get him to the festivities, Sergio drove up to the hotel in gleeful anticipation. This was going to be so much fun!

Inside the hotel, most of Sergio's classmates were already in full party mode. Squealed greetings, warm hugs, and fond laughter joined in with '80s rock hits played by a raucous band.

Even though the room was already fancy, the reunion planners had topped off the room with streamers and a big "Welcome Class of '85" banner that hung high on the wall. Reunion attendees talked and joked and danced under a floating cloud of helium balloons.

When the ballroom doors opened to let in the latest arrival, all eyes turned to see who was coming in now. In unison, all those eyes widened in horror.

The music stopped playing with the screech of a discordant guitar chord and the reverberating clash of a cymbal. Talking ceased entirely. The entire room went completely silent.

Then a woman screamed. And another. And another.

One woman fainted.

Someone threw up.

Several people covered their mouths. Several more turned away. Some started running toward the back of the room.

Not sure what was causing the upset, Sergio looked behind him to see if something terrible was coming. He saw nothing. A man and a woman were at the far end of the hall, but they were headed the other way. A waiter was coming out of another ballroom, but he, too, was going in the other direction. No one was behind Sergio.

As Sergio started to turn back toward his classmates, his gaze landed on the floor.

He frowned. The floor was disgusting! What had happened in this hallway?!

Sergio hadn't noticed the floor when he walked in, probably because he was so eager to make his captivating appearance. But now he stared at it.

The gold carpet behind him was stained with a thick trail of blood. No, not just blood. White bits of flesh nestled in the blood. He also saw what looked like bone bits, clumps of hair, and blobs of what appeared to be pink spongy tissue dropped at intervals along the center of the hallway. The blobs gleamed in the glow from the overhead chandeliers and seemed to wiggle as he looked at them. It was nauseating.

Sergio was appalled! He thought this was supposed to be a classy hotel!

Someone should do something about the mess, but if he went to get a hotel employee now, he'd mess up his timing. His classmates were waiting for him.

Sergio looked back down the hall to where he'd left Lucky Boy sitting on a chair so he could watch Sergio's triumph. Lucky Boy would agree that Sergio deserved to have the best cleaners take care of this mess.

Lucky Boy giggled.

Sergio looked down at his feet and noticed even more gruesome waste staining the carpet next to his brand-new shoes. Oh, for heaven's sake! Some of the gore had even gotten on the black leather. He leaned over and wiped off what looked to be some rubbery gristle.

He shook his head. He would deal with the hotel's janitorial shortcomings later. He turned back to his fellow classmates.

"Now," he said to himself, "where is Sophia?"

Hudson leaned his gangly six feet, one inch against the cracked brick archway just inside the newly constructed Fazbear's Fright Horror Attraction. The archway was only two weeks old, but it was made to look like the crumbling entrance to a place thirty-plus years forgotten.

Hudson watched his buddies, Barry and Duane, carry in the latest batch of Fazbear memorabilia for display in the endless halls and rooms inside the building. The lobby was already piled high with opened and unopened cardboard boxes, each stuffed with vintage finds from various Freddy Fazbear's restaurants.

Hudson was doing his best to stay away from the boxes, or not the boxes, actually, but what was *in* the boxes. The management had dubbed them "vintage finds," but as of a couple days ago, Hudson was calling them something else.

The boxes, as far as Hudson now was concerned, were full

of old creepy stuff. And it was old creepy stuff that gave Hudson the heebie-jeebies . . . because he didn't believe it was just *stuff*. No matter how he tried to rationalize, the memorabilia made the little hairs on the back of his neck stand up stiffer than the needles his granny stuck in voodoo dolls.

"Hudson, think you could give us a hand?" Barry asked.

Hudson's buddies were struggling to keep a stack of boxes upright, but Hudson didn't move.

"I'm not part of the construction and setup crew. I'm the guard."

Duane spit on the linoleum floor. The disgusting blob of saliva landed right in the middle of one of the black squares, which alternated with white squares to create a dizzying checkerboard pattern throughout the building. The floor gave Hudson a headache.

The whole building was giving him a headache.

How did something that had started so right now feel so wrong?

"I'm the guard," Duane mimicked Hudson in a whiny singsong voice. "You hear that, Barry? He thinks he's entitled or something."

Hudson snorted. "Yeah, right. I'm entitled to working double shifts—days *and* nights—and you guys get to work days."

"Whine, whine," Duane said. "This is the best job you've had in years. You said yourself the pay is great."

Hudson nodded. That much was true, and he'd thought the job would have even more than great pay to offer. But ever since . . . no, now it was just a job with crap hours, and he was tired all the time. "Sure, but sleep deprivation tends to make you stop caring about great pay. I have to have some perks for holding the short end of the stick. One of those perks is getting to stand here and watch you two sweat."

"Fine. Be like that," Duane said as he and Barry finally steadied all but the top box in their stack. When that box fell, Barry managed to catch it.

The box popped open when Barry grabbed it. A yellow furry arm flopped out. Hudson stiffened. Oh man, how he hated those character parts. They were the worst of the creepy old stuff, for sure.

Barry set down the box. Duane pulled out the arm, then reached in and grabbed a second arm. "Check this one out," he said. He held up the second arm and looked at what it held.

"What the heck is that?" Barry asked.

"I think it's a cupcake," Duane said.

"Not a cupcake I'd want to eat," Barry said. "Look at those teeth."

Duane started toward Hudson with the two arms, pretending to be a fuzzy-yellow-armed zombie. He made guttural groaning sounds as he staggered across the room.

Hudson held his ground and pretended to be bored, but the truth was that he wanted to scream and run. The disembodied arms were bad enough, but the cupcake was just disturbing.

Hudson pulled out his nightstick from the loop on his belt. He made like he was going to have a sword fight with Duane's zombie. He thought he was doing a pretty good job of acting playful and relaxed, and he hoped Duane didn't see the sheen of sweat on his forehead or smell the pungent scent that was starting to emanate from under his arms.

Wait . . . was that smell his? Or was it coming from the disembodied arms?

"Cut it out, you two," Barry said. "How old are you?"

"Twenty-three," Duane said. "Same as you. Are you having memory lapses in your old age?" Then he laughed and returned the arms to the open box.

Barry and Duane left the building to return to the truck for another load. Hudson strolled nonchalantly down the hall until they were out of sight. Then he strode to the office, the real office. There, he went in and shut and locked the door.

Dropping into the cheap, wobbly desk chair in front of a bank of monitors, Hudson surveyed the building, starting with the fake office. Fazbear's Frights was being set up to be a sort of expanded replica of the Freddy Fazbear's restaurants. Not a true representation of any one of the actual old places, this attraction spliced together aspects of the infamous pizzerias with all the murderous history. The office was one of those aspects—the place where hapless security guards like Hudson managed to miss seeing the tragedy as it unfolded so many years ago.

The fake office had already been decorated by the attraction's design team. They'd done a good job of making the room look old and dingy, mostly because they were able to use salvaged derelict equipment original to the old pizzerias. Clunky monitors, dusty keyboards, bent filing cabinets, and a scratched desk had been shoved into the room. They then covered those surfaces with piles of paper, wadded-up trash, paper cups, and a crooked old fan that squeaked as it ran. They even let loose a rat or two in the room. The rats apparently were pretty tame and had a place to stay, tucked into a vent in the wall when they didn't want to "perform." But when they scurried around, they gave Hudson the willies. He figured more than one girl would scream her head off when the rats appeared. Hudson had nearly screamed himself a couple times. He wasn't a fan of rats.

And speaking of the vent, it was one of the small functional vents for the heating and cooling system. Higher up on the wall, huge louvered vent covers made it clear the vents behind them were massive, certainly large enough to accommodate a good-size man, or something not so ordinary. Hudson, who was tall but skinny, could have easily had a picnic inside one of those vents if he was so inclined, which he wasn't. *What in the heck were those big vents for?* Hudson had asked the question, and he hadn't received an answer. That unsettled him. He didn't think the vents were for anything good.

Hudson noticed movement on the monitors, and he leaned back in his chair to watch Barry and Duane carry in another load. Both men were laughing. And why shouldn't they laugh? Barry and Duane had it made. Unlike Hudson, they were good-looking, respected around town, and on the verge of going into the Navy to train for a spot on a SEAL team.

When Hudson, Barry, and Duane were boys, they were the Three Musketeers, ready to take on the world, invincible, unstoppable. Hudson could remember the swashbuckling "fights" they had in their backyards. Reenacting scenes from their favorite action movies, they didn't have a care in the world.

But that was before Hudson's dad died and his mom married Lewis, a ridiculous balding man who wore plaid vests and smoked a pipe like he was giving a performance every time he took a puff from it. To this day, Hudson couldn't stand the smell of cherries because Lewis had used black cherry pipe tobacco.

This horrible little man Hudson's mother thought it would be a good idea to marry would make Hudson's next ten years a living hell. The day his crazy mother said "I do" to Lewis was the day life started saying "I don't" to Hudson. It was also the day when his life path and that of his best friends started to diverge.

Sure, they all remained friends. They still had fake sword fights. They still hung out. But everything else changed. Barry and Duane did well in school, so their parents were proud of them, and they did well in sports, so they were popular with the other kids. While their stars were on the rise, Hudson began to screw up in class, a product of spending the night in fear that his stepfather was going to bust into his room and beat him just for the fun of it. Sore because of the near-daily beatings and malnourished because his mom started taking pills to get her through the day and therefore forgot to do mundane things like grocery shop, Hudson couldn't get on a baseball or football team to save his life.

Barry, whose red hair and freckles had been awkward when he was young, became an auburn-haired novelty to the cheerleaders and fans alike in high school. Duane, who wore tight black shirts to show off his muscles and grew his black hair long enough to wear in a glossy ponytail, was like walking catnip to girls. Even though Barry and Duane still tried to include Hudson, there was no place for him, really, in their world.

And so it went, year after year, until the night of the fire.

And then, just when he was sure his troubles were over and the sun was finally going to rise again in his life, things just got worse. To have that happen again here, in this new job . . . it wasn't fair.

Pounding on the office door jerked Hudson from his pathetic stroll down memory hell. He scrambled upright.

"What?" he shouted.

"We're going to knock off and go to Charlie's for a sundae in fifteen minutes," Barry called. "Coming with?"

Hudson looked at his old, scuffed watch. That would work. He got six hours off between shifts, just enough time to get ice cream, go home, eat canned soup, then try and sleep for four hours. What a life.

"Sure," he called.

"Meet us out front."

"Okay."

Hudson sighed and stood. He had to do one more walk-through before he passed the keys to Virgil, the old guy who covered for him when he went home. Hudson was pretty sure Virgil didn't do a thing but sleep while he was here. But Virgil wasn't Hudson's responsibility. Hudson just wanted to do a good job on his shift so he could keep the better pay coming in. It wasn't like he had a lot of job options available.

That thought made him grind his teeth.

"Thanks, Lewis," he muttered as he left the office.

In the hallway, he took a deep breath and gave himself a little mental pep talk about what he had to do.

This is not rocket science, he thought. *Nor is it an advance into enemy territory, a fight with deadly demons, or a descent into hell. It's just a tour through a building that has a lot of old creepy stuff.*

When the goose bumps popped up on his forearms, he knew his usual pep talk had failed. No amount of reasonable assurances could make a dent in his new, utterly illogical fear of this place.

Hudson put a hand on his nightstick and began whistling as he headed away from the office. He made sure to stay in the middle of the hall as he walked toward his least-favorite part of the building. He stayed in the middle because the walls of the hallway were already "decorated."

The entire interior of Fazbear's Frights, although in a brand-new building, had been made to look like a long-abandoned space. Already dark and gloomy because it was nearly windowless (only the tiniest of windows were set high up on the walls), the rooms and hallways looked ancient because painters had used all sorts of weird techniques to create walls that looked dirty, mildewed, and cobweb-covered. As if that wasn't bad enough, the designers had begun covering the mottled walls with decayed, time-ravaged bits of Fazbear characters. Hanging in netting or from strings, sometimes nailed to or impaled on the wall by knives, the hallway walls were lined with parts of old Fazbear character suits and animatronic parts like wires and joints. The main attractions were the whole costume heads of three of the characters: Freddy, Foxy, and Chica. These had positions of prominence in the hallway, but interspersed with them were a cornucopia of character pieces: bunny ears, bear paws, chick feet, fox snouts, fuzzy purple bellies, matted furry brown legs—these were just a few of the spine-chilling slices of Fazbear lore that waited in the hallway to startle unsuspecting passersby . . . or to grab them.

Hudson had heard that the designers were working on animating several of the hands. It wasn't functional yet, but once, Hudson's arm had brushed a purple bunny hand as he went by, and he'd beaten the hand into the ground before he realized he was pummeling an inanimate object. Luckily, he'd been able to reattach the hand to the wall, and, apparently, the designers hadn't remembered the hand wasn't that mangled when they'd put it up.

Interspersed with the character parts, images of pizzas and children's drawings created a feeling of disorientation. So did the thick, torn electric cables dangling from various parts of the ceiling. They looked like headless black snakes. They weren't live electric cables, of course. At least, Hudson assumed they weren't. He wasn't about to touch one and find out.

At the end of the hall, Hudson sighed in relief and then set his shoulders before he stepped into his least-favorite room in the building: the dining room. He always checked this room first to get it out of the way.

When he was hired, Hudson thought this was going to be a great gig. Yeah, the hours sucked, but not only was the pay great, the job also came with the chance to get to know the lovely dark-haired petite girl who was going to art school and working here part-time with the design crew. Faith—she even had a lovely name—was every bit as nice as she was pretty, and she was new in town. This meant she didn't know Hudson's history. Which also meant that she didn't hate him on sight. And that meant she actually laughed and joked with him as she flitted about, tucking the odd bits of animatronic parts in with old Fazbear plates and cups and party hats on long tables covered with torn purple tablecloths.

As Hudson had helped Faith carry boxes all over the building, Faith had told him about her little sister and her dog, Goose, a spaniel—a bird dog that was afraid of geese. Hudson had loitered nearby while Faith painted sets all over the building, and she'd told him about her car, Bettina, a classic MGB that she spent her weekends working on.

"You know engines?" he'd asked her, thinking for sure she was the perfect woman.

"Do I know engines?" Faith had laughed. "I could build you one."

Hudson had grinned at her like an idiot.

Faith laughed harder. "I also like sports." She stopped laughing and smiled at him. "I like you, too. So, why haven't you asked me out?"

After he'd blushed redder than the fake blood Faith was painting the walls with, he asked her out. They went out for pizza. He thought he'd died and gone to heaven.

But it was too good to be true.

Hudson barely waited five hours before calling Faith to ask her out on a second date, but that was too long. In that five hours, somehow, Faith had heard about him. When she answered his call, she'd asked, "Did you do it?"

All the good feelings he'd had about her drained from his body like someone had turned a valve that emptied joy out through his big toe. He was pissed. Why did people always have to ask him that question?

"What do you think?" he snapped.

Faith was quiet for a few seconds. Then she said, "I think we should be more professional on the job."

Hudson didn't even respond. He just hung up the phone.

Ever since then, the job had gotten on his nerves. And so had the building and everything in it.

Now, as he stood in the dining room Faith had designed, he wondered at the ghostly jump scares and grizzly reminders of old crimes never quite forgotten. Where did she get off judging him for something he might or might not have done?

Her mind was clearly twisted. How else could she have come up with the idea of a door opening and a hand reaching in to drag a little boy out of sight?

Hudson stared at that feature of the dining room, then ran his gaze over the place settings on the table and the animatronic parts placed in bizarre positions on the chairs. He studied the statues on the stage, created to look like the original animatronic animal performers that used to sing and entertain at the original Freddy Fazbear's restaurants. The statues were, unlike their inspiration, completely non-functional. They couldn't move on their own.

So why did Hudson always feel like they were watching him?

Hudson left the dining room and went through an archway into the arcade area, although calling it an "arcade area" didn't really describe it. It looked more like an arcade junkyard. Hudson thought the management had exhumed every old, broken, dirty, cobweb-covered arcade game that used to lie in a landfill to bring them here. Hudson had seen an actual worm crawl out of one of the pinball machines the day before.

Beyond this game cemetery, a pile of rotting prizes cascaded out into the adjoining hall. Some of the prizes were in morbidly wrapped packages (think bloodstains and images of bones mixed with characters' eyes and teeth). Some, looking every bit as decrepit as the arcade games, were lying loose on a broken, dusty counter or on the floor in piles. These "prizes" could no longer be called prizes. They were more like punishments. Maybe he'd be allowed to hand them out to kids who didn't behave themselves when the place opened.

Hudson, eyeing a headless baby doll, grinned. He would find a sick sort of enjoyment in handing out hideous "gifts" to kids. Kids were nearly always mean to him. Maybe he could get a little payback.

Chuckling, Hudson turned away from the "prizes." He continued on his last security tour of this shift.

He turned down one long hall and then headed up another; took sidesteps into fake storage, wardrobe, and supply closets; switched back through the replica of a pizzeria kitchen—complete with working industrial-size ovens so big Hudson would fit inside them, until at last he completed his rounds. He ended up near the building's lobby. There, he stepped into the bathrooms, first the men's and then the women's. He tried to avoid glancing in any of the mirrors when he was inside the ridiculously bright red spaces. Hudson didn't like looking at himself.

It wasn't that he looked bad. He figured he looked pretty normal: short blond hair, three day's growth of a pale beard, blue eyes, a wide mouth full of straight white teeth—these weren't features to be avoided. But to Hudson, these features added up to one thing he never wanted to face: himself. Facing himself meant facing his past. He could only manage that in snippets.

Stepping out of the women's restroom, Hudson paused near the gift shop that sold an amazing assortment of Fazbear merchandise. The store had a little of everything Fazbear related. The animatronics were no longer in one piece and functioning, but their images were displayed on hundreds of items. Visitors were going to be able to buy plush toys, action figures, clothing and accessories like Chica hair bands and Freddy hats, housewares that included sheets and towels, artwork, sporting goods, and greeting cards based on the old characters.

The gift shop was about three-fourths of the way stocked, and he knew it was supposed to be a bright and cheery place, with its red-and-yellow-striped walls and its colorful posters of the Fazbear characters. But he thought the rows and rows of little eyes on the plush toys and action figures were anything *but* cheerful. He thought the hundreds of small characters looked like they were lining up for an invasion of some kind. He didn't want to be around when that invasion came.

He knew from horrific personal experience that toys could turn from fun to instruments of torture in a heartbeat. Of course, that required—

"There you are," Duane called. "You ready to go?"

Hudson looked out the front door of Fazbear's Frights and spotted Virgil getting out of his thirty-year-old Ford sedan. Hudson nodded. "Ready."

He couldn't wait to get out of here, even if was just for a few hours.

Since they were kids, Hudson and his friends had been going to Charlie's, an old-fashioned soda fountain and ice-cream parlor on the other side of town. Although they should have outgrown the place a long time ago, they all liked going back to it from time to time . . . not just for the ice cream, but for the reminder of an innocent time they had all left behind. Well, at least Hudson and Barry had left it behind. Hudson wasn't sure about Duane. And it was usually Duane's idea to come here.

Hudson liked the place, but he didn't like going to the far side of town; it meant he had to bum a ride from his friends. And he'd have to bum a ride back. It sucked having no car.

It sucked having no life.

Hudson and his friends arrived in the narrow, dimly lit, wood-paneled parlor filled with red-leather stools and booths. Hudson surveyed the scene. "This place is starting to look a little like Fazbear's Frights. It needs a good cleaning."

Duane slid into a booth and stretched out his legs. "Who cares? Doesn't this place make you feel like a kid again?"

Barry and Hudson squeezed in opposite Duane. Barry

snorted. "It would take more than an ice-cream parlor to make me feel like a kid. And you? What do you mean 'again'? We're all still waiting on you to grow up."

Duane grinned. "You say that like it's a bad thing." The small ice-cream parlor only had a couple other customers—a teenage couple sharing a float. As they sucked their concoction through a straw, they stared into each other's eyes.

Hudson glanced at them, then fixed his gaze on the chrome jukebox on the black-and-white checkerboard floor at the far end of the room. It was way too similar to the one at Fazbear's Frights to suit Hudson. Zoning out, he reflected on his younger self, trying to remember the last time he'd felt truly happy.

It was weird. He could perfectly envision his pre-Lewis days in his mind, but he couldn't feel them. It was like watching some other kid's life on a movie screen in his head.

Sighing, he drew a deep breath. The room smelled like dust and furniture polish. Only a hint of sweeter scents, like vanilla and cherries, managed to get through to his nostrils.

"Barkeep," Duane bellowed, "three of your finest."

The guy behind the soda fountain wasn't one they recognized. He was muscular and had a buzz cut. He rolled his eyes at Duane.

Duane laughed. "Oh, all right. Three chocolate sundaes. Hold the cherries."

Hudson leaned back and half listened to Duane and

Barry talk about the day while he watched the sundaes being made.

When the sundaes arrived, Duane and Barry argued over the bill. Hudson noticed neither of his friends asked him to pay. Not that he could have. After he paid his rent and utilities this month, he'd have exactly $123.67 left to buy groceries and pay for bus fare to and from his job. Better pay was a relative thing. He was still poor.

If only the Navy had wanted him, like it had wanted his friends.

Of course, it hadn't. How could he hope to pass a physical? He had two fused disks in his spine, left over from when Lewis threw him against a wall after he mouthed off to him. He had a wrist that gave him fits; it hadn't been set right after Lewis crushed it under his boot because Hudson wet himself during a thunderstorm. Not to mention the nerve injury. He was damaged goods, barely able to walk the spooky halls of Fazbear's Frights.

"I shouldn't be eating this," Barry said, digging his spoon into whipped cream, chocolate syrup, and vanilla ice cream. "Dinner at my grandparents' house this evening."

"Chicken-fried steak and white gravy, mashed potatoes, and creamed corn?" Duane asked.

"What else?"

"Gotta love grandmas," Duane said, spooning ice cream into his mouth. The rich aroma of chocolate cut through the dust and polish smells.

"You got that right," Barry agreed. "Yours does that incredible apple pie, right?"

Duane nodded. "And cinnamon rolls. Thankfully, she only visits a couple times a year. I'd be a tubby if she lived close like yours."

"How's your granny, Hud?" Barry asked. "You haven't mentioned her in years. Is she still alive?"

Hudson nodded and grinned. "I don't think she can die."

Duane nudged Barry. "You remember how afraid you were of her when we were kids?"

Barry held up his hands. "Hey, I'm not ashamed." He looked at Hudson. "What reasonable person *wouldn't* be afraid of your granny?" He laughed.

Hudson smiled and nodded. "Only an idiot would cross her."

Duane grinned. "Remember when she made that voodoo doll of Mr. Pikestaff?" He laughed. "The jerk walked funny for a week, and she only used two pins."

Hudson smiled again. His granny was not your run-of-the-mill grandma.

"That was a good one," he admitted. "But I've always thought Granny was more wise than scary. She's always known stuff." He thought about how creeped out he'd been feeling at Fazbear's Frights. "Like she always told me that if the hair stands up on the back of your neck, you should do what it wants and stay alert because trouble's coming."

Duane laughed. "So what's got the hairs on the back of your neck standing up?"

Hudson looked at him. "For real, you want to know?"

Duane said, "For real."

Hudson didn't speak. Instead, he thought about his granny.

An expert in the use of herbs to heal whatever needed healing, Granny Foster was a seer who claimed to know the future but never bothered to tell anyone else about it. She didn't have any particular faith or belief system, including voodoo, but she thought voodoo dolls were "a hoot," and she liked using them to mete out justice to unpleasant people.

"Why, Granny?" twelve-year old Hudson asked her once. "Why do they work for you, when you don't even believe in voodoo?"

Granny Foster, who always wore big men's plaid flannel shirts with baggy jeans, rocked in her chair on her front porch, and said, "I believe in what I believe, and because I believe it, it works for me."

"I don't know what that means," Hudson said.

"You don't know what you believe. That's why life knocks you around the way it does."

Granny Foster had a lot of pithy pronouncements like that, and Hudson had spent years thinking about every one of them. It was one of the reasons he was so edgy at work.

"Earth to Hud," Duane said.

Hudson blinked. "Sorry." He took a bite of his ice cream. "Okay, what makes my neck hair stand up is Fazbear's Frights."

Duane laughed. "Really? That place? There's nothing hair-raising about it. It's just smoke and mirrors for schmoes who think being artificially scared is a good idea."

"Like there isn't enough real scary stuff in life to keep us busy," Barry grunted.

"Exactly," Duane said. "Fazbear's Frights is just a place to work. It's a job. A short stop along the road."

"Maybe for you." Hudson sighed. "You're not stuck here."

Duane scooped up more ice cream and didn't respond, but Barry said to Duane, "He has a point."

Duane shook his head. "You can't think that way, Hud. You have to believe things will break for you."

"Things break all right," Hudson said, thinking about his attempt to date Faith.

"I mean break in a good way," Duane said.

"I know what you mean."

Barry and Duane dropped Hudson off at his basement studio apartment four hours before he had to catch the bus to get back on the job. A little drowsy and a lot hungry, Duane put a can of chicken noodle soup on the tiny stove to heat. While he waited for it, he stared at the noodles and thought about his mom the way she was before Lewis came into their lives, before Hudson's dad had died. She'd never been a particularly warm and fuzzy mom, but she'd been efficient and responsible . . . until her husband was gone.

Hudson's dad, Steven, had been one of those dads every kid wanted. Always up for throwing the ball, playing a game, or just roughhousing, Hudson's dad was fun and attentive. Unfortunately, he also struggled with mental illness for many years. For every happy, high-flying adventure his father had taken him on, there were many more invisible low points that he'd hidden. When Steven got himself into a bad deal that cost him his small business, and thus his family's livelihood, he'd taken his life.

Over the years, Hudson had vacillated between loving his dad for the childhood memories they'd shared, and hating him for leaving Hudson and his mom alone and destitute, easy prey for a monster like Lewis.

Hudson also spent a lot of time asking himself if he was prone to the same bad luck as his dad. Maybe he was, or maybe he just let his dad's fate seal his own.

Hudson wasn't sure what had happened, but for some reason, after his dad was gone, everything went wrong. It wasn't just about Lewis or about Hudson's weak, checked-out mom. It was everything.

Suddenly, for instance, he became a target for the worst bullies at school. He was locked into supply closets before class and chased home after the last bell rang. He was pushed, shoved, punched, and almost drowned when his head was held in a flushing toilet. That happened more than once. One of the bullies called him "Swirly-Head."

The teachers at school weren't much better than the bullies. When Hudson's grades started dropping, no one stepped up to help him. No one wanted to know why his grades were going south. They just wanted to yell at him for not keeping up. One, Mr. Atkin, a tough algebra teacher, even called Hudson stupid in front of the class.

And the sad thing was that school was the *easy* part of

his life. Home was much, much worse. Lewis had a daily reminder for Hudson: "You're nothing." The word, *nothing*, was alternated between beatings. "You're nothing." Slap. "You're less than nothing." Punch. "You're smoke."

Now, there was some irony, given what eventually happened.

Granny Foster liked to say that heat and fire purged. And she was right . . . sort of.

When his family's house burned down at the end of his senior year, it purged Hudson of Lewis and his mother. But it didn't purge his torment. That just worsened.

The problem was that the fire investigators concluded the fire wasn't a natural fire. Given Lewis's known violent proclivities, Hudson thought the police would immediately suspect his late stepfather of the crime. Instead, they turned their eyes on the stepson Lewis knocked around.

For five years, Hudson had been free of Lewis, his mother, and his teachers. But while Duane and Barry had been away at college, he'd gone from one dead-end, boring job to another because he couldn't shake the stigma of being a suspect in an arson/murder. When his friends got back, they started taking high-paying temporary jobs in construction or whatever, basically just having a good time for a bit before they had to get serious about life. Hudson had been a clerk at a local convenience store for the previous six months until Duane and Barry talked him into applying to Fazbear's Frights. The idea was the three of them would hang out together at Fazbear's for a few weeks and then join the Navy.

A fine idea . . . if Hudson hadn't been battered into worthlessness.

Hudson took a deep breath and noticed the smell of something burning. He looked down. The soup broth had boiled away, and now the chicken and noodles were blackened and stuck to the bottom of the pan.

Hudson snatched up the pan and threw it in the sink. Smoke filled the air and stung his eyes.

How long had he been standing there feeling sorry for himself?

He looked at his watch. *Too long.*

Sighing, Hudson ran water in the pan and got out a scrub brush. After cleaning up, making a new can of soup, and eating, he'd only have three hours to try to sleep before he had to get back to work.

Virgil was waiting just outside the gift shop when Hudson got back to Fazbear's Frights.

"Any issues?" Hudson asked Virgil.

"Not unless you call this place's busted thermostat an issue," Virgil said.

Hudson shook his head. The building never felt cold to him. "You need to get your wife to knit you a thicker sweater."

Virgil tugged at the threadbare cardigan he wore. "Nah. I like this one. It's comfortable."

Hudson nodded, then waved goodbye to Virgil as he shuffled out the front doors. As soon as he was out, Hudson locked the doors.

Turning to face the building, Hudson listened to the silence that surrounded him. Weirdly, the silence seemed to move around him like a living, breathing entity. It seemed to have layers, nuances that contained information he didn't understand. No, not just information. Threats. The silence felt like a threat, like a promise of something unpleasant to come.

Hudson pressed his back against the closed door and tried to control his quickening breath. He resisted the temptation to unlock the door and run out into the night.

Somewhere in the guts of the building, something thumped. Hudson drew his nightstick.

Then he laughed at himself when he felt cool air pouring from the nearest floor vent. The sound he'd heard was just the cooling system cycling on.

"You need to get a grip," he told himself.

He took a deep breath and blew it out slowly. Then, keeping his nightstick in his grip, he set out on his rounds.

Darkness stretched out ahead of Hudson as he walked his usual route. The building's lights were set to dim after midnight, causing the boxes stacked in the corridors to cast unusual shadows. Memorabilia that had been unpacked threw shorter, fatter shades that reminded Hudson of the rats in the fake office. When one shadow seemed to shift, he pulled his flashlight and shined a beam on the area, wondering if one of the rats had gotten out of the office.

Or maybe they'd brought in more rats. He wouldn't put it past them.

After three weeks of keeping an eye on the place while

it was being prepared for the public, he was getting used to the rapidly evolving interior. Unfortunately, each room got more unsettling as time passed.

The problem was with all the weird characters.

Whoever had thought of Freddy Fazbear's characters had a crazy imagination. Who came up with things like a chick with teeth carrying a similarly toothy cupcake? Who thought up purple bunnies and foxes with eye patches? And who came up with the black-striped marionette mask that was painted like a warrior? Hudson didn't even want to know what the rest of that character looked like. Just the mask hanging over one of the doorways was bad enough.

And, of course, Faith and her cohorts had played up every element of Fazbear freaky weirdness. Fake blood was artfully splashed about. Cobwebs and dust and scratches had been added to every surface—not just on the walls.

Apparently, in addition to the coming animations, they were going to be adding sound soon. Very soon.

Hudson had to assume the sounds would be turned off at night, but he wasn't sure if that was the case. He wondered how he could keep his sanity if he had to listen to Fazbear sound effects in addition to seeing the disturbing sights.

Maybe once the boxes were gone it would get better. Something about those boxes was disconcerting. He didn't know what lurked inside of them. What was coming out next?

After he'd gotten past the fake office, the janitor's closet, and the kitchen, Hudson did a sweep through the dining room, and checked the stage, doing his best to stay out of arm's reach of the character statues. He knew that was silly. They were *statues*, not animatronics. But he couldn't help himself. He just felt like they were going to grab him if he got too close.

Hudson checked behind the stage. He noticed more animatronic suit parts had come in. They were scattered across the floor and hanging on the walls. Blood (*aka red paint . . . remember that*, he told himself) had been flung across many of the suit parts.

Leaving the backstage area, he went down a few of the meandering hallways until he got to Pirate's Cove. Faith had told him that Pirate's Cove was in the dining room in the restaurants, but she wanted to make it a separate space here.

"I mean," she said when she was still talking to Hudson, "imagine the fright it will give people when this pirate's hook slashes through the curtain over and over?" She giggled.

Hudson didn't think it was funny.

He was glad Foxy's head, with one eye covered by a black eye patch, was disconnected from the rest of the character suit. He hated to think about a functional character—be it a human wearing a suit or an animatronic—that controlled the lethal-looking hook.

Leaving Pirate's Cove, Hudson moved on to the fake office. There, he discovered a bin of character parts and props had been added. He could see the neck of a rock guitar sticking out of the disembodied heads. A loaded trash can had been shoved into the room as well. One of the rats was digging into the garbage. Hudson quickly shut the door and moved on.

Completing his circuit and ending up back in the lobby, under the "crumbling" brick archway, Hudson looked at his watch. It was only 1:50 a.m. He had over five hours to go before Virgil would come back to relieve him for a few hours. Virgil was supposed to come in at seven, along with Barry and Duane, but he was usually late.

Hudson tapped his nightstick against his thigh. Time to go hide in the real office and watch the monitors for a while.

Hudson entered the office and put his nightstick back on his belt. He holstered his flashlight and sank into his chair. This room was Hudson's sanctuary. It was the only place in the building where he didn't feel like hundreds of eyes were on him.

The only thing in the office that made him nervous was the huge vent cover high on the wall above his desk. A couple days ago, he'd decided that someone . . . or something . . . could easily watch him through that louvered cover. So, he'd brought an old blanket from home and tacked it over the vent cover. So far, no one had said anything about it. He wondered if Virgil ever felt like he was being watched through the vent. Hudson never asked him.

Hudson leaned back and put his feet up. He settled in to wait for the night to pass.

When Hudson returned from his short break the next day, it was nearly noon. Barry and Duane were carrying in another tower of boxes, and Faith was sitting on the floor pulling all sorts of new "vintage finds" from the cardboard containers.

"We're breaking for lunch in fifteen," Duane called to Hudson as Hudson entered the building. "Will you be in the office?"

"Sure." Hudson figured he could fit in his starting circuit in that time if he hurried.

Even though he and his friends weren't as close as they used to be, he still found their company comforting. It made him feel just a little less alone in the world. He didn't like to think about what it would be like after they shipped out.

He'd miss the camaraderie . . . and the stupid jokes. Duane was always telling really bad dad jokes.

"What do you call wood when it's scared?" Duane asked as he and Barry came into the office at the same moment Hudson was returning from his rounds.

Hudson said, "I don't know. What?"

"Petrified." Duane barked out a laugh.

"Corny." Barry shook his head.

Hudson chuckled.

Barry took out a bag and crossed the room to where a small microwave sat on a shelf. "Guess what I brought you guys."

"Food?" Duane asked.

"Funny. Not just any food. Chicken-fried steak with white gravy, mashed potatoes, and homemade creamed corn."

"Will you marry me?" Duane asked Barry. "Anyone who marries you gets your grandma in the deal, right?"

"Sure, but you're not my type."

"What is your type?" Hudson asked.

"Not you," Barry said.

All three men laughed.

Barry stuck the food in the microwave and turned it on. Immediately, the nearly intoxicating aroma of chicken-fried steak filled the room. Hudson realized just how hungry he was.

"Speaking of marriage," Duane said to Barry, "how'd your date with Faith go?"

Hudson stiffened. Barry went out with Faith?

"Great," Barry said. "Really great. She's pretty amazing." Barry looked down at his hands and then looked at Hudson. "She said you two went on a date once but it didn't work out. Are you okay with me dating her? I won't if you're not."

Hudson shrugged. "Sure. I'm okay with it. I'm not dating her. I'd have to be a world-class jerk to say you can't just because I went on a date with her."

"What happened?" Duane asked.

Hudson rolled his eyes. "What do you think?"

Duane and Barry looked at each other. "We didn't tell her," Barry said. "We don't talk to anyone about it."

Hudson shrugged.

Barry opened the microwave and pulled out the steaming plastic containers. He started parceling out the food on paper plates.

Hudson was trying not to be mad at his friend, but he didn't think he could bring himself to accept his charity on top of everything. "None for me," Hudson said. "I'm not hungry."

"You sure?" Barry asked.

Hudson nodded.

Barry shrugged but left some food in the containers. "I'll leave your share here for when you get hungry later."

Through a mouthful of mashed potatoes, Duane added, "Unless I get to it first."

Barry handed Duane a napkin. "Close your mouth. Didn't your mama teach you any manners?"

Hudson looked past his friends and checked the monitors. He noticed the stacks of boxes had grown higher in the lobby.

"How much more stuff are you two bringing in?" he asked.

"We were told there are a couple more truck-fulls coming in," Barry said. "Some big find is arriving tomorrow."

"What kind of find?" Hudson asked.

Duane shrugged in response.

"I don't care about more finds," Hudson said. "When is the phone system being put in?"

"Day after tomorrow, I think," Barry said. "Faith said she wanted to get a couple more projects done before that team came in."

Trying not to imagine Faith and Barry together, Hudson shifted his gaze from one monitor to the next. He shook his head at all the junk being crammed into the building.

"What's wrong?" Duane asked.

Hudson shrugged. He didn't want to get into sharing his feelings with his friends.

"Whatever you say," Duane said.

"I didn't say anything," Hudson said.

Duane licked his plate. "Whatever."

"You know you look like a dog when you do that," Barry said. "Right?"

"Don't care," Duane said. "It's good." He put down the clean paper plate and looked at Hudson. "What's up with you the last few days? You've been acting weird."

Hudson shrugged. "When Faith asked me if I did it, it brought it all back, you know? Messed with my head."

Barry cringed. "That's why I asked if you want me not to see her."

"You like her?" Hudson asked.

"I do."

"Well, then, date her."

"We'll be gone in a couple months," Duane pointed out.

Barry shrugged. "No one can predict the future."

"Granny can," Hudson said.

The men laughed.

When his shift break came later in the day, Hudson declined his friends' invitation to dinner. He needed to go see Granny.

"You need a ride?" Barry asked.

"I'll walk," Hudson said. He'd decided he wouldn't even try to sleep this evening. He'd visit Granny, get her to feed him, and then see if she had something for boosting his energy. If anyone could keep him awake, it would be Granny.

So Hudson left Fazbear's Frights behind at 5:00 p.m., and he strode the ten blocks to his granny's place. The day was cool but dry. The first of the fall leaves skittered along the concrete in front of him as he walked. He inhaled the scent of crab apples, which had fallen from trees by the sidewalk. Granny had told him scents have power, and when a scent is appealing, inhaling it will give you strength. "Don't inhale putrid smells," she warned him once. "They're more than just smells. Everything is more than it seems."

Just shy of the modern apartment building that housed his granny, Hudson caught a scent of something rotting. He covered his mouth with his hand and jogged into the building as some young hip businessman was coming out.

When you thought of a granny like Granny Foster, unconcerned by appearances, who followed "the old ways" and who used voodoo dolls to handle conflicts, you didn't think of finding that granny in an ultra-modern, open loft apartment.

When Hudson was a kid, Granny Foster had lived in an old house near where Hudson and his parents lived. By the time of the fire, though, Granny had moved. She said the energy was better downtown. And the place was closer to men. Granny Foster had started dating.

Hudson grinned as he took the sleek black elevator up

to the sixth floor of the old warehouse that had been converted to lofts. Thinking about Granny Foster dating always cheered him up.

Hudson had never met Grandpa Foster. He'd died before Hudson was born. It was hard to imagine a man strong enough for the likes of Granny Foster. So far, none of her dates had gotten even a semipermanent position.

Hudson stepped off the elevator, listened to the *ding* as it closed behind him, and strode over a polished cement floor down the far end of the hall. Someone on this floor was baking cookies. They smelled like sugar cookies. He was sure that someone wasn't Granny. Her idea of baking didn't result in something as yummy as a cookie.

Two steps before Hudson reached Granny's door, it opened. Granny was wearing a red-and-green plaid shirt with her baggy jeans. "You're late."

Hudson hadn't told her he was coming.

He chose to ignore her words. He leaned over to hug her. She smelled like exotic spices . . . and peaches. He inhaled.

Granny Foster's power didn't come from her size. She was only five feet, one inch. And she was as skinny as Hudson was. He'd have been concerned about breaking her when he hugged her if he hadn't learned over the years that she had a power that was much stronger than her barely encased bones. Nothing was going to break Granny Foster.

A fan of being out in the sun, Granny Foster's skin was dark and thick like cracked leather, and she'd had wrinkles layered on wrinkles for as long as Hudson could remember. She'd also had wild jaw-length hair that was always in disarray. Her hair was white; apparently her hair had turned white when she was not much older than Hudson was now. He'd never asked her why. Somehow, neither the wrinkles nor the white hair made Granny appear old or weak. Combined with her sharp features and unusually bright blue eyes, they made her look tough, which she was.

When he let her go, Granny Foster kicked the door shut and motioned for Hudson to follow her. Instead of leading him to the black leather sofa by the wall-to-wall window that looked out over downtown, she led him to the center of the room and pointed.

"Is that a fire pit?" Hudson asked, staring at the small, stone-walled circle with the burning coals within.

Granny waved a hand. "Fake. But it will do."

Her voice did not match her body. Deep and gravelly, Granny's voice belonged in a trucker's body. It was one of the reasons she was scary. When she spoke, her guttural tones sounded like a demon was controlling her and using her body to speak to helpless humans.

"Well, aren't you in a snit?" Granny said.

Hudson said nothing. He'd learned that speaking as little as possible was the best way to interact with Granny. You had to wait for her to say whatever she was going to say and then go away and try to figure it out later.

"Sit." She pointed at an orange pillow on the floor by the fire pit.

Hudson sat.

"It's wafting from you like you rolled in excrement, Hudson. You have to let it go."

"How?"

"Leave it."

"What?"

"The job." Granny dropped her eighty-two-year-old body into an impressive-for-her-age cross-legged position. "You need to leave that job, Hudson."

Hudson frowned. He thought so, too, but he also thought his thoughts were the ravings of an idiot. He was making more money than he'd ever made before . . . not that it was enough yet, but it was a step in the right direction. What was he going to do? Go back to making minimum wage and dealing with all the jerks who came into the convenience store? Who treated him like he was a piece of gum stuck to the bottom of their shoes?

"I can't, Granny," he said.

"Mm."

Hudson thought about Granny and her predictions. Maybe she knew something.

"Why should I quit?" Hudson asked. "What do you know about Fazbear's Frights?"

She squinted at him. "All I need to know." She reached out and squeezed his hand. "I care about you, Hudson. Quit your job."

There she went again. Saying nothing substantive. It was just more of her silly voodoo. Hudson shook his head. "If I give in . . ." He shook his head again. "I can't."

Granny sighed. "Your path is your own." She held his

gaze for several minutes. Then she popped up. "Come on. Let's have pizza. I'll call it in."

Hudson grinned. "Sure, why not."

That night at Fazbear's Frights passed without incident, and Hudson was so relaxed when he went home after his shift that he actually went to sleep and stayed asleep for five hours. He returned to his job late in the morning, just in time to watch Barry and Duane unload a coffin-size wood crate from their truck and carry it inside the building.

Accepting the key ring from Virgil, Hudson trotted up the front steps of the building and watched his friends carry the box down the hall.

"What is that?" Hudson called out.

"Come and see," Duane said. "It's going to be mind-blowing. You won't believe where this was found."

Hudson hooked his keys on his belt and followed his friends.

"Where are we going?" Hudson asked.

"The inner hall," Barry directed. "That's where they want it."

"Get this," Duane said. "This was found inside a hidden room in one of the pizzerias!"

Barry smiled. "Faith is really excited about it. She said they're going to put it in a hidden room here now, and it's going to be the best feature of the whole attraction."

Hudson looked down at his nightstick and adjusted it so Barry wouldn't see how flushed his face was. "Is she here now?" Hudson asked as casually as he could.

It must have sounded good because Barry just as casually replied, "No. She's spending the day shopping for fabric and paint or whatever to go with this new prop."

While they talked, Barry and Duane grunted and shuffled their way down the long hall. It didn't occur to Hudson to offer help. He was too busy thinking about Faith to be thoughtful.

He noticed the hallway was free of boxes in this section. More character parts had been added to the walls. He thought there were at least a dozen or more new pairs of eyes peering out from the walls.

Barry and Duane dropped the crate on the linoleum with a resounding thud. Hudson flinched, sure he heard, on the heels of the thud, a metallic sound coming from inside the crate.

Duane plopped his butt on the crate and wiped sweat from his face with the hem of his T-shirt.

"I left the crowbar near Pirate's Cove," Barry said. "I'll go get it."

"You're not going to open that, are you?" Hudson asked.

"What?" Duane asked. "Don't tell me you're afraid of what's in this box." He looked up at Hudson. "You think we haven't noticed how jumpy you are around this stuff? You're letting this weirdness"—he waved a hand around at the walls—"get to you. And that's your choice, man, but you're giving in to the power of suggestion. Basic psychology. What you expect is what happens. Self-fulfilling prophecy and all that. I know you took psych, too, Barry. Remember the experiments they did that proved that what you see when you look at things in the world depends not as much on what's actually there but more on the assumptions you're making when you look at things. Remember?"

"Sure," Barry said, "but it's not for you to tell Hudson—"

Hudson touched Barry's arm. "It's okay." He kept his face nonchalant and said, "I need to go on my rounds." He strode away, but he could hear Barry talking as he did.

"You can be a real jerk, you know that?" Barry said.

"What did I do?" Duane asked, sounding genuinely baffled.

Of course, he wouldn't get it. Duane, as far as Hudson knew, had never been afraid of anything in his life. He was always the first one to jump off the roof when they were trying to "fly," always the first one out on the ice to check the pond for ice-skating, always the first one to charge into a fight to break it up on the playground. Barry was no slouch at being courageous, either. He once got a $1,000 reward from an old lady when he climbed a hundred-foot tree to rescue the woman's cat.

And Hudson? What had he done? He'd hid from Lewis instead of fighting back.

Hudson shook himself mentally and stomped down the hall to do his rounds.

A half hour later, Hudson was on his way to the office when Duane called to him. "You have to come and see this thing. It is creeptastic!"

"Leave him alone," Barry said.

"Oh, come on. It's not a demon. It's an old animatronic, a whole animatronic! It's amazing. Look at the detail!"

Hudson wanted nothing but to go to the office, shut the door, lock it, and take a nap. But he wasn't going to give Duane the satisfaction. So he strolled down the hall as if he couldn't care less about what was in the crate.

When he reached his friends, he stopped dead. Trying to wrestle the animatronic upright and get it propped against the wall, Barry and Duane had their arms around the most bizarre-looking thing Hudson had ever seen.

Right. *Bizarre.* He was using that word because using the word *terrifying* would mean that he was afraid. And he *was* afraid, but he sure didn't want to admit it to anyone, including himself.

Hudson called on an old trick he'd used when Lewis was on a rampage. He narrowed his eyes until his focus was almost down to a pinpoint. He'd learned when he was young that when your perspective was that narrow, what you were facing wasn't as horrifying.

Using that pinpoint focus, all Hudson could see propped between Barry and Duane was a set of white staring eyes with heavy green lids. That was enough to freak Hudson out.

But it was also a small enough part of the thing his friends were wrestling with that he could act relaxed and unconcerned. Testing that theory, he spoke. "What are you doing with it? Dancing?"

His voice sounded normal and light. He congratulated himself.

"Faith wants the thing standing here against this wall," Barry said. He grunted and shifted his side of the life-size animatronic. "Did you get those hooks attached?" he asked Duane. "Or are you just going to flirt with it?"

Duane pulled a couple hooks out of his pocket. "You hold your side in place. I'll lean against my side, and I'll attach the hooks to the wall. Then we'll switch places and set up the other side."

"I'll leave you to it," Hudson said, turning to go to the office.

"Want to go for dinner after work?" Barry called out.

Hudson stopped and looked back. "I can't. Sorry. Virgil isn't coming in this evening. I'll be here until tomorrow morning."

"Sorry," Duane said. "Sucks to be you."

"Thanks for that," Hudson said, shaking his head.

"I'm just sayin'," Duane said.

"Maybe the SEALS can teach you not to stick your foot in your mouth," Barry said to Duane as Hudson was walking away.

Hudson fully expected to have an easy night of it. In spite of the addition of the new animatronic, he was feeling good when he closed the building up for the night. Maybe pretending to be relaxed was actually making him feel more relaxed. He figured he could make the self-fulfilling prophecy thing work for him.

And it did . . . until he decided to poke the bear; that was when he got all courageous and resolved to face his fears.

He'd spend the rest of the night paying for it.

Normally, Hudson did his rounds in the same direction and the same order. But tonight, he was eager. So he started at the end, intending to reverse his usual direction. This brought him to the new animatronic near the beginning of his circuit, instead of the end.

As he approached the scruffy thing, he planned to face it right off and get it out of the way. He was going to rob it of its power to upset him.

Good plan, but he forgot to squint his eyes.

And he wasn't planning on the thing talking to him, either.

Hudson strode down the inner hall, and he found the new animatronic hooked to the wall just where Duane and Barry left it. Posed in a friendly hand-up-to-wave position, the animatronic's posture wasn't threatening. But really, anything that looked like this *was* threatening, no matter what it was doing.

Hudson faced the animatronic, then stumbled back and sucked in his breath. What in the world was this thing supposed to be?

At first glance, the robotic character attached to the wall appeared to be a rabbit. Sort of. With fur of greenish yellow, this was no ordinary rabbit, though not even a cartoon rabbit. It was the kind of rabbit Dr. Frankenstein might have created if he'd wanted to build a rabbit instead of a man.

Ears torn, dozens of pieces of the body's and limbs' yellow-green fur ripped away . . . or chewed away—it was hard to tell—this was a rabbit that would never be cuddled by any child. It shouldn't have been *seen* by a child, either.

Where the fur was torn, you could see metal pieces of the animatronic's structure. Exposed wires linked to an oxidized metal frame and . . . something else. What was that?

Hudson couldn't help himself. He leaned in to get a better look.

Was that?

No, it couldn't be.

He studied the reddish and grayish areas that could be seen through gaps in the fur and metal. It looked like . . .

Hudson took a step back and clutched at his nightstick. He realized he was breathing too fast, and he bent over to get a grip on himself.

He needed to go back to squinting. But he couldn't. He had to know.

Stepping closer again, Hudson tilted his head to get a better look at what was hiding under the fur and metal. He was going to show himself that his crazy flight of gruesome fancy was just that: fancy.

But it wasn't. Hudson lifted a finger and carefully extended his hand far enough to touch what was inside the ravaged fur and the exposed metal. He put the tip of his finger against the reddish material.

And he jumped back so fast he lost his balance and fell against the opposite wall.

It was! It was tissue. Maybe not, no, probably not *human* tissue. But it was some kind of bodily tissue.

Who would want to terrify someone with gore like this? It couldn't be real!

"It's real," a scratchy voice said.

Hudson scrambled back.

It spoke! The animatronic spoke?

No, that wasn't possible. Duane and Barry told him the thing was completely nonfunctional. Experts were going to be brought in to work on it, and even then, they figured it was beyond repair.

"If you weren't so stupid, I'd tell you more about it," the voice said.

The voice was distinctive, way too distinctive. A base voice with a burr-like rasp, the voice had a hint of a Southern accent.

Hudson knew that voice.

It was Mr. Atkin's voice.

Hudson drew his stick.

How could Mr. Atkin's voice be coming out of this thing?

Or *did* the voice come from the animatronic? No. Hudson didn't think so.

The voice seemed to fill his head, coming more from inside his ears than outside of them. He couldn't pin down a direction.

"Who said that?" Hudson asked. He looked around, then looked back at the animatronic. It hung on the wall, its tooth-filled mouth completely still.

Hudson turned his head to look up and down the hall.

"Stupid," the voice said again.

Hudson whipped his gaze back to the animatronic's mouth. It was exactly as it had been before.

Hudson stared at the mouth for several minutes. The voice didn't speak. The hallway was silent.

Hudson blinked and looked down the length of the animatronic, staring at the jagged lower edge of the fur ending above exposed ankle . . . bones? Were those bones?

Nah. That *was* stupid. They had to be metal supports discolored by age.

"Do the math," the voice said.

The voice, and the word *math*, brought back a rush of memories from Mr. Atkin's algebra class. Hudson could suddenly smell the chalk in the classroom, feel his sweat-dampened jeans sticking to the hard seat of his desk. He could feel his classmates' eyes on him, feel Mr. Adkin's disdain. He wanted to run away and hide.

Tears welled in Hudson's eyes, but then he remembered he wasn't a child anymore. He felt a surge of anger, and he shoved his nightstick in the animatronic's mouth. He heard a snap, a tinkle, and a clatter on the floor. He'd broken off one of the animatronic's teeth.

Or had he?

Was that tooth there when he first approached the thing?

"This is nuts," Hudson said. He reached out and grabbed the animatronic. His intention was to carry it to a closet and lock it inside. But the thing was heavier than it looked, and it wouldn't budge from the wall.

"What kind of hooks did you use?" Hudson asked the absent Duane.

He peered at the connections, and he couldn't figure out how to release them.

Well, okay. This was good, right? This meant the animatronic couldn't go anywhere.

Hudson set his shoulders, turned, and strode down the hall away from the abomination hanging on the wall. He might have heard a whispered "Stupid," as he went, but he wasn't sure, and he decided to pretend he hadn't.

Instead, he marched into the dining room to do his rounds properly, from the beginning. Striding past the tables, he thought about that voice. He hadn't heard that voice in over ten years. He hadn't thought about Mr. Atkin in that amount of time, either.

Why was he suddenly hearing a voice that sounded like Mr. Atkin? Was someone playing a prank on Hudson? Would Duane and Barry do that?

Duane maybe. But not Barry.

"Let it go," Hudson told himself. Maybe he'd imagined the whole thing.

He had gotten himself totally worked up about this place in the last few days. He'd never taken rejection well, and his disappointment in Faith (who did not live up to her name) could have caused a little emotional crash and burn. Maybe his mind was tormenting him because *he* was tormenting himself for not handling Faith's question better.

What would she have done if he hadn't gotten

defensive? He could have just said, "No, of course I didn't do it."

Or what if he'd just said, "Did what?" all innocent and made her explain her question?

He could have said, "That's not an easy question to answer." That would have been the most honest thing he could have said.

Would she have gone out with him again if he hadn't snapped at her?

"Stop it!" Hudson admonished himself. Going through these what-ifs and should-haves was like beating his head against a brick wall.

Hudson went through the archway and started passing the crippled arcade games. Since he was already carrying his nightstick, he beat a rhythm on the metal and plastic and wood as he passed the game remains. He did this every night; it broke up the tedium.

Tonight's drumming session wasn't typical, though. As he drummed, Hudson swore he could hear singing. He stopped drumming, and the singing stopped.

Who was singing?

Hudson took a step back and looked around the dining room. His gaze slipped past the characters on the stage, and then it jerked back.

The characters. They'd moved since he'd passed them.

The singing started again.

And the characters' lips were moving.

They were singing!

That was not possible. They were statues!

Hudson went back in the arcade and started rapping his nightstick more loudly on the games. He was determined to drown out the impossible singing.

Before Hudson could rap on the third game in the line, though, he got another surprise. This one was not as benign.

Suddenly, Hudson's nightstick was ripped from his grasp and thrown across the room. It hit the wall with a *thwack* at the same time Hudson's head slammed down . . . onto the scarred wooden desk under the window in his bedroom.

"Why isn't your homework done?" Lewis bellowed.

The impact was powerful, and the corner of the desk that contacted with Hudson's temple was sharp. So he was hit with the double whammy of searing pain and a blinding stream of blood flowing down into his eyes. Stumbling back, Hudson swiped at the blood, trying to clear his vision so he could see Lewis enough to know what the man was going to do next. Lewis had been hitting Hudson for years, but this was the first time Lewis had slammed his head into something.

As Hudson wiped his eyes, he rotated, staggering. But he didn't see anyone. Where was Lewis? He was gone.

Hudson was alone in the arcade.

Wait. What just happened?

Pressing his hand to the bleeding wound at his hairline, Hudson blinked at the arcade game in front of him, a bent and crooked alien invaders–type game. He saw blood on its metal frame.

He wasn't in his bedroom. Lewis didn't just slam

his head into a desk. His head had been slammed into the game.

Hudson looked for his nightstick. He couldn't find it. And he couldn't stop the bleeding with his hand. He had to get back to the office. He had a first aid kit there.

But was it safe? Something really weird was going on. Why did he hallucinate a scene from his childhood?

A muted *thud* sounded from a few feet away.

"Who's there?" Hudson shouted.

He held still, listening. He heard nothing but his hitched breathing. He tried to ignore the pounding in his head so he could think.

Blood trickled down the hand Hudson held to his head. Whatever happened, he needed to bandage his wound. He couldn't just stand here.

Retracing his steps through the dining room, Hudson scanned the area for a threat. But it was too dim and well shadowed for him to have a clear view of every part of the room. The tables, chairs, muted lighting, and cast shadows provided too many hidey-holes for anyone who might want to attack or torment Hudson. Besides, he knew no one was there anyway. He was alone in the building.

Which made what just happened all the more distressing.

Still bleeding, Hudson rushed through the room. Then he jogged down the hall toward the office. He made it there without any trouble.

After closing and locking the office door, Hudson checked all the monitors before awkwardly wiping blood from his wound and covering it first with gauze and then with surgical tape. While he doctored himself, he tried to ignore the pain throbbing at his temples, and he tried not to think about the monitors showing no movement of any kind in the whole building.

Hudson finished his first aid efforts and sank into his chair. He looked at his bloody hands, then got up. He had to go to the restroom and get himself cleaned up.

He looked around the room. Without his nightstick, he felt exposed and vulnerable. He needed a weapon. He spotted a hammer he'd forgotten to return to the supply closet after he'd used it to fix his desk a couple days before. He picked it up, hefted it, swung it, and nodded, satisfied. This would work.

He took a breath, checked the monitors again, and turned toward—

Wait.

He looked back at the monitors. He blinked and rubbed his eyes.

His vision was a little blurry, probably from both the blood in his eyes and the blow to the head. Was he seeing that wrong?

He leaned toward the monitor in question.

No. He wasn't seeing it wrong. He was seeing what he was seeing.

Where was the animatronic that was supposed to be latched, immobile and trapped, to the wall in the inner hall?

Hudson flung the office door open. Gripping the hammer so hard his knuckles turned white, he strode down the hall to the—

Oh hell.

It *was* gone. It really was gone.

Hudson gawked at the empty hooks hanging from the wall.

Hudson heard a scuffling sound behind him. He whirled.

Nothing was there.

Or *was* something there, hiding just past that pile of character suits?

Hudson pulled out his flashlight and shined it around the hallway.

No. He didn't see any movement.

He took a step down the hall, moving toward the bathroom. Turning in circles constantly, he tried to be aware of the entire hallway at once. He wished he had eyes in the back of his head.

He made it to the men's bathroom without further incident. Pushing the door open, he tensed and raised his hammer. Who knew what was lurking in here? Was the mutilated rabbit waiting for him?

Hudson snorted at the word *rabbit*. He was thinking of the animatronic as a rabbit because it made him feel better to think of it being about as threatening as a teddy bear. But, of course, that was ignorance.

"Stupid," the Mr. Atkin voice said.

Hudson whirled.

He was alone.

Again, he couldn't tell where Mr. Atkin's voice came from. Because it *was* his voice. Hudson was sure of it.

For once, Mr. Atkin was right. It was stupid to think of

the animatronic as a rabbit. It was as much a rabbit as Hudson was. No, the abomination that Hudson's friends had so calmly installed this morning was not a rabbit at all. It was a robot. And it was more. Hudson was pretty sure the remains of a corpse were stuck inside the rabbit-suit skeleton. He wasn't one-hundred percent convinced, but he was convinced enough.

Quickly checking to be sure all the stalls were empty, Hudson held the hammer with one hand while he splashed water on his free hand. He quickly realized this was a clumsy way to clean up that wasn't going to work, and after double-checking the room, he set down the hammer and started to wash his hands in preparation for cleaning up his face.

He never should have set down the hammer.

Hudson went from standing still to backpedaling toward the handicap-accessible stall in a half blink of a second. He was by the sink. And then he wasn't. Now he was skidding across the bathroom, hauled by unseen hands toward the toilet in the biggest stall.

Hudson screamed, "Stop it!" and tried to grab at the stall doorway as he went through it. He couldn't get a grip on it to stop his progress.

He slid the few feet to the toilet.

"Hold him down!" one of the boys shouted. "Get his shoulders," another one yelled. Hudson got one last glimpse of the gray linoleum floor of the boy's bathroom before he felt his head going into the toilet. He closed his eyes and his mouth just as he was submerged.

Then the water swirled to the sound of laughter.

Hudson flailed and thrashed and fell back into the closed door of the stall. He coughed, spit, and tried to upchuck what little food he had in his stomach.

Water sluiced down his neck and trickled under his shirt. "Get away from me!" he screamed at the bullies tormenting him, even though he knew that yelling would spur them to do something else to him.

He tensed, bracing for another assault.

Nothing happened.

Hudson looked around. His gaze fell on the floor . . . the black-and-white floor.

He squinted at it, then put a hand on it. No gray linoleum.

His upper lip curled at the scent of urine. Hudson hefted himself to his feet, fumbled with the stall door, and bolted for the nearest sink. He stuck his head under the faucet and scrubbed at his face and hair with the hottest water he could stand. When he was done, he used a pile of paper towels to dry himself off as well as he could.

Then Hudson looked back into the stall he'd just exited. He stared at it. What was wrong with it? Something wasn't right.

Hudson took a step back. Then he took two steps forward.

No, that wasn't possible.

But it was.

The toilet in the stall and the stall floor were completely

dry. And it smelled the way the rest of the bathroom smelled—like soap and disinfectant.

If he'd just whipped his head out of a urine-filled toilet, water would be splashed all over, and the stall would still have that acidic putrid scent. How could the stall look suddenly pristine?

Hudson couldn't make sense of this, and it made him angry.

"Think you've gotten me, don't you?" Hudson shouted.

He didn't know whom he was shouting at, and that made him even angrier.

"What do you want?" he screamed to whom or what he didn't know.

No one and nothing answered.

Hudson breathed heavily for several seconds. Then he sighed. "Okay. I give."

He wasn't sure what it was going to accomplish to give in to his opponent . . . who *was* his opponent? But maybe acting meek could buy him some time to figure out what was going on. Ha! *Acting* meek? He wasn't acting at all! He wanted to surrender, wave the white flag, and roll over on his back like a submissive puppy. He wasn't up for whatever kind of warfare he was in. He didn't understand it, and he wasn't equipped for it.

Speaking of which . . . He picked up the hammer.

He didn't want to stay in the bathroom all night. He might as well head back to the office. He took a step.

He stopped when he heard a chuckle.

That was a chuckle, right?

Yes. There was another one.

Now he was being laughed at.

Where was the laughter coming from?

Sounded like it was coming from above him. Hudson looked up.

Sure enough. There was the source of the laughter. The yellow-green rabbit's head was hanging out through the opening of the big vent high on the wall.

Its mouth was open, and it was laughing its head off.

Hudson roared and threw his hammer at the tooth-filled head.

The head disappeared back into the vent.

Hudson stared at the opening. He had to pursue. Didn't he? First, if he didn't pursue, he'd know he was a coward. Second, how would he know where the rabbit went if he didn't follow it? If he didn't know where it was, he was in more danger.

Before he could think more about it, Hudson jumped up onto a toilet seat, climbed onto the pipes, then to the top of the stall door. He grabbed the lip of the vent and heaved himself up into the cavernous tube above the ceiling. Once there, he went rigid, expecting further attack.

Nothing happened. He pulled out his flashlight, flipped it on, and shined it around.

He was alone.

He stopped and sat in the giant vent. What was he doing in here? This was crazy. Did he really want to go after the animatronic rabbit?

Hudson straightened his shoulders. Yes. Yes, he did.

He wasn't going to be a sniveling kid anymore. He was going to stand up to the bullies and his miserable stepdad. He was going to go rabbit hunting.

Hudson giggled at his joke.

Did his giggle sound a little demented to his own ears?

Wasn't he slipping in and out of his present and his past? For a second, he was a kid pretending he had the courage to go after the bullies who hurt him.

But it was just a second. He knew where he was. And he knew he had to go on the offensive or he was going to lose his mind.

Getting onto his hands and knees, Hudson put his flashlight in his mouth and crawled away from the opening to the men's restroom. Stopping every few feet to take the flashlight from his mouth and aim it this way and that while he listened for sounds, he got about twenty feet before he encountered his first character head.

Startled, he lifted his own head and bumped it on the metal above him. He scuttled backward and stared at the face looking back at him.

It was Freddy Fazbear himself.

Not really. It was a Freddy costume head, an old, nearly threadbare one. Or was that *threadbear*?

Hudson giggled again, and he had to admit the giggle was too childish sounding.

He needed to focus on the task at hand. Find the escaped rabbit. No. Find the bullies. No. Find the strange animatronic.

He scooted forward to a vent corner. He peered around

the corner, and he spotted another head. Again, he jumped so violently he banged the top of his head against the metal above him.

He forced himself to breathe calmly as he studied the head. It was Chica's, though her teeth were half gone, and her bill was torn.

This head was still attached to part of Chica's body. The body had just a shoulder, an arm, and a hand.

Hudson gave the thing a wide berth, watching it to be sure it wasn't going to suddenly grow feet and come after him. He didn't stop watching until he rounded a corner.

Hudson didn't know how long he crawled through the vent system. He also didn't know how many heads he found. He lost track of both time and sensory input. Every stretch of the vent seemed like every other. Every turn was both familiar and unfamiliar. Several times he was sure he got a glimpse of yellow-green fur up ahead. Each time, he stiffened and readied himself for an attack, but one never came.

Twice, Hudson heard the scrabbling of little claws on the metal in the vent, and he spotted one of the rats. He found rat droppings, too.

"Gross," Hudson said more than once when he put his palm on rat poop.

Sometimes when he stopped moving, Hudson was sure he heard swishing sounds or tapping sounds or clinks or bumps from ahead or behind him. Mostly, though, he heard his own breathing—his own ragged, labored breathing.

Finally, his knees sore and his head throbbing and

tingling, he decided he was never going to win a game of hide-and-seek in these vents. And he had to get back to the office and rewrap his head.

So, he turned to crawl down a vent tunnel that went toward light. He wasn't sure where he was in the building—he'd gotten totally disoriented—but he was sure he had the leg strength to kick out a vent cover, and because the vent openings were so huge and the ceilings weren't unusually tall, he figured he could drop from the vent opening to the ground no matter where he came out.

He began crawling ahead.

But something grabbed his foot.

Something grabbed his foot . . . and held on.

Swallowing a scream, Hudson turned and looked behind him. He fully expected to see nothing because he kept seeing nothing when he turned to check sounds.

But this time, something was there.

Screaming, Hudson yanked his foot toward his body and sat up. Once again, he bashed the top of his head against the vent tunnel ceiling, but he didn't pause to care about it because the thing hanging on to his foot was still hanging on.

"Get off!" he screeched. "Get off!"

Using his flashlight, he beat at the yellow arm that had a grip on his foot.

It was Chica again . . . the Chica head attached to a shoulder, arm, and hand. And the hand was hanging on to Hudson's foot as if his foot was the most important thing in the world.

Hudson shook his foot and pounded on the yellow hand that wouldn't let go.

"I like you," a woman's voice said. Not just any woman's voice—Faith's voice.

Hudson froze.

He shined his flashlight back and forth in the vent tunnel. Then he aimed the light at Chica's mouth. Had the voice come from Chica?

"I like you," the voice said again.

The voice didn't sound like it was coming from the Chica head. Just as the Mr. Atkin's voice had come from a void Hudson couldn't locate, so did this one. This voice, however, had a more immediate impact on Hudson. He felt it squeezing his heart, touching him the way it had when Faith said those very words to him on their first—their only—date.

"I like you," Faith had said.

It was a different "I like you" than the casual way she'd said the words at work before she basically told him to ask her out. In the restaurant, under the muted lights in the alcove where their small table was tucked, Faith's eyes had looked so soft and sincere when she said it. And it wasn't *just* "I like you." What she actually said was "I like you a lot, Hudson. You're a nice guy."

And then she reached across the table and touched his hand. Her fingers were so smooth and warm. And when he turned his hand over and took hers in his, she didn't protest. She just smiled at him in a way no one had ever smiled at him before.

It was the best moment of his life.

Unlike this one.

Now Hudson wasn't in the restaurant with Faith. He was in the huge vent, with a piece of an animatronic glommed onto his foot.

Aware of the pressure still grasping his foot, Hudson tried to lean forward and use his fingers to pry Chica's hand from his shoe. But that was a bad move . . . because Chica just shifted her grip. Now she was holding his right hand.

Faith hung on to Hudson's hand when he walked her home. She smiled the whole time, too. She listened to him, laughed at his jokes, and at one point, she even put her head on his shoulder for a moment. A strand of her hair blew up against his neck. It felt so silky, and it smelled like berries.

Hudson welcomed the warmth, the connection. He looked down at his hand, entwined with—

It wasn't Faith's hand in his.

"No!" Hudson screamed.

He no longer felt touched, not emotionally anyway. Obviously he was being *touched,* literally, by the yellow hand. And maybe he was touched in the head, too.

Hudson swung his arm around, which in turn swung the Chica parts around. He battered them over and over against the vent tunnel's sides. Chica was oblivious. She held on.

He had to get out of here. Doing his best to not think about the animatronic part attached to his right hand,

Hudson crawled ahead, making for the vent cover he'd had his eye on. He knew if he could get out of the relatively confining vent space, he'd have more room to maneuver Chica off his hand.

Ignoring Chica's continued expressions of determined love, Hudson crawled to within a couple feet of the vent cover, turned his body, and kicked the cover loose from the wall. Crawling forward, he shined his light down into the room below. He was backstage.

Wow. He was totally turned around. He'd thought he was on the opposite side of the building.

Turning again, Hudson exited the vent tunnel feetfirst, dropping to the floor and immediately swinging his arm in a wide arc to slam Chica against the floor. When her grip loosened, he flung her free and kicked her into a pile of costume parts on the far side of the dressing area.

"I like you," he heard again.

And then he heard a sound he'd never heard before. It was a sound he could barely describe.

It was a roar, he thought at first, an especially shrill roar with distinctive separate tones that told him it was a combined roar, the combined roar of many, many voices. It was also a breath, a great exhale, and a groan all at once.

"What—?" Hudson began.

The costume parts began to tear the Chica parts to bits. Like a frothing, churning pool filled with fuzzy, colorful piranhas, the costume parts came to life, and in seconds, they pulled Chica apart and ripped her into a hundred pieces.

He would have kissed Faith good night by her door after their date, but her roommate opened the door and walked between them just as he was making his move. Later, after Faith called to ask if he'd done it, he realized the roommate had opened the door and walked out deliberately to keep him from kissing Faith. That was probably the moment when it all began to come apart.

As quickly as the attack on Chica began, it ended. The pile of costume parts was once again just a pile of parts. It didn't look any different than it had before.

And now Hudson was looking at wisps of yellow fabric. Chica had been reduced to almost nothing . . . just like Hudson. Faith's rejection had torn his heart and his hope into little bits.

He looked at his hands. Was that yellow fuzz under his nails?

Hudson wiped his hands on his pants several times.

And once again, Hudson was alone in the stillness. Not liked. Not capable of understanding what was going on.

Hudson turned away from the yellow tufts of fur. He ran back toward the office.

When he reached the end of the hall, however, he stopped. He looked down at his empty hands. He'd lost his nightstick. He'd lost his hammer. With the animatronic wandering somewhere in the building and with everything else going on—what *was* going on?—he needed a new weapon.

He veered away from the office, in the direction of the kitchen.

When Faith and her team first designed it, the kitchen was only going to be a replica of one of the pizzeria kitchens. But then management decided they wanted this attraction to be available as a venue for parties. That's when the fake kitchen became a real kitchen.

Over the last few days, Barry and Duane had been bringing in boxes of kitchen supplies. They were still stacked up next to the counters. Surely one of those boxes contained a knife or something that could be used as a weapon.

Hudson reached the kitchen without anything else weird happening, and he found what he needed in the second box he opened. Continually checking over his shoulder, Hudson armed himself with a butcher knife and a rolling pin.

Feeling only a little ridiculous as he left the kitchen, he held both weapons ahead of him as he hurried back to his office. Twice along the way, he was sure he heard a *clickety-click* behind him, but when he checked both times, nothing was there.

Finally reaching the office, Hudson looked around it thoroughly before closing and locking the door. Then, setting down his weapons, he tore off the wet wrap on his head. He used the remainder of his bandages to rewrap it because his head was still oozing. When he was done, he sat down in his chair.

Hudson checked both the monitors and the blanket hanging over the vent cover. Nothing was amiss.

What should he do next?

Hudson looked up at the ceiling, then shook his head.

The solution was so easy he couldn't believe he missed it.

"Stupid," Mr. Atkin said from somewhere.

Hudson groaned. He *was* being stupid. He didn't have to stay in this building and be abused all night.

"Just plain stupid," the Atkin voice said.

Hudson stood. All he had to do was get out of the building. Why was he still in here? It wasn't like he was locked in. He had keys.

He reached down and touched his key r—

He looked down. Where were his keys?

Oh no. The belt loop on which he normally hooked his keys was torn. The keys were gone.

He looked madly around the room.

Checked his pockets.

Looked at the monitors.

No keys.

"Stupid," the Atkin voice reminded him.

Hudson closed his eyes and hung his head. If he'd gone for his keys first, he would be out of here by now.

He opened his eyes. Well, there was nothing he could do about that now. Unless he could break out somehow, he was locked in. He couldn't call anyone, either. He had no phone, and of course, the building's phone system was coming in *tomorrow*.

But why not break out? Sure, he couldn't easily reach the few windows in the building, but couldn't he break the glass front doors?

Maybe. Or he could just wait out the night in here. He was safe in here . . . or at least he'd know if someone or something was trying to get in.

The second he had that thought, something thumped against the door.

And the blanket over the vent rippled. The vent made a rending sound, and the vent cover fell down from behind the blanket to land with a clatter on the floor.

As soon as the vent landed, animatronic mouths and costume mouths began falling though the opening.

"What's the square root of 144?" Mr. Atkin asked.

No, not Mr. Atkin.

An animatronic mouth.

"What?" Hudson said.

"Wrong. Stupid!" Mr. Atkin said.

It was Mr. Atkin in his algebra class. Hudson could see the windows looking out at the school parking lot, the cars glistening in the rain.

"What's 4x + 6?" Mr. Atkin said. "Work the problem."

Hudson looked around. He wasn't in algebra class. He was in his office. Animatronic mouths surrounded him, firing algebra questions at him.

Hudson held his head.

"Stupid!" another mouth said, using Mr. Atkin's voice.

"How do you find a value through the process of substitution?" Mr. Atkin screamed through another animatronic mouth.

Hudson shook his head and willed himself to see what was real and what wasn't.

"Stupid!" a different mouth said.

All the mouths sounded like Mr. Atkin.

"Stop it!" Hudson shrieked. "Stop it!"

All the mouths advanced on him.

"Stupid."

"Stupid."

"Stupid."

"Stupid."

The assault came from inside and outside of his head. And it came from all around him as the mouths fell endlessly from the vent opening and pressed toward him in a ghastly chorus of judgment.

Hudson tried to get up and run, but the mouths were like marbles flung all over the floor. He lost his balance and fell.

And then they overran him. Mouths crawled all over him. They skittered up his legs, slithered through his hair, and hopped from one end of his body to the other.

Hudson flailed and kicked. He shrieked some more.

When a mouth tried to crawl inside *his* mouth and another one began to burrow into his ear, he started hearing rumbling in his head, like a thunderstorm was unleashing itself inside of him. That's when he lost it.

He wet his pants.

As the hot liquid left his body and soaked his jeans, he began to cry. He was babbling, too. He didn't know what he was saying. He was talking gibberish.

He was in a world of misery beyond anything he'd experienced before. And that was saying a lot.

Wrapping his arms around himself, he began to rock and hum.

He didn't know how long he rocked and hummed, but when Hudson stopped, the mouths were gone.

Completely gone.

Like they'd never even been there.

He looked around then looked up at the blanket. It was hanging in place, and it was thick enough to cover the opening so he couldn't tell if the vent cover was there.

He started to stand so he could move the desk and check the vent cover, but that was when he noticed the sticky burning wetness in his pants. Oh man, he had to get cleaned up. He wasn't going to sit in his own pee the rest of the night.

Hudson picked up the butcher knife and the rolling pin. Pausing to listen at the door, Hudson slowly opened it. Hearing nothing, he stepped into the hall . . . and he tripped and fell toward the floor.

No. He was grabbed.

He was grabbed by the wrist and flung, as if he was half his size. The wrenching motion of the grab and fling broke the same wrist Lewis had broken when Hudson was a boy.

Or *was* he still a boy? Hadn't he just felt Lewis's clammy palm against his skin? Yes, he'd seen the green shag carpet in the hallway of his house flash past his gaze as he flew through the air.

"You peed your pants, crybaby?" Lewis boomed. "Pathetic."

Hudson moaned as he landed. He cradled his snapped wrist against his belly, and he gasped in siren-like yelps as he looked around.

No green shag carpet. Still the black and white squares. He wasn't at home. He was in Fazbear's Frights.

And he'd just been flung. And he'd just lost his butcher knife. It was lying a few feet down the hall, still spinning— the black end pointing at him, then the pointed end, then the black end, then the pointed end.

Again, he was alone.

Well, not totally alone. All the animatronic parts on the walls were muttering. They were whispering, giggling, pointing, reaching, and, worst of all, *watching*. He could see the eyes on the wall following his movements.

Hudson gasped. Two of the reaching arms had weapons. One had his nightstick, and one had the hammer. Both arms swung their weapons back and forth. A partial Foxy arm, with its pirate hook extended, was between Hudson's two weapons; but the hook was unmoving.

Hudson forced himself to look away from the chaotic movement on the walls. It was making him dizzy. Or was he dizzy because of his broken wrist?

Tears smeared Hudson's face as he dropped the rolling pin and tried to get up without affecting his left wrist. Even the slightest hint of a movement sent red hot streaks of pain down into his hand and up his arm. It felt like his wrist was a raging bonfire.

Managing to get into a sitting position, Hudson, without thinking, started to scoot back against the wall. That was when the sharp end of Foxy's pirate's hook cut through the material of his shirt and scratched his back. He yelped and used his right hand and his legs to move away from the writhing walls. Once there, he tried to brace himself with his right hand in the middle of the hallway floor, but then he realized he needed his right hand for self-defense. He leaned forward, grabbed the rolling pin, then sat still, trying to get control of his sobbing and his hiccupping breath.

On either side of him, parts still reached and grabbed.

No, *Lewis* reached for him.

Hudson was sitting on the green shag carpet, cradling his wrist.

"Get up, you sissy!" Lewis screamed at him. "Get up!"

Hudson hunched over, trying to make himself smaller than he already was.

Between his knees, he saw . . . the black-and-white floor. He dared a glance around. The walls still wanted him, and he was barely out of their range.

He tried to think about what he had to do next.

He looked around for the knife. It was a few feet down the hall. He didn't have the strength or the will to get it.

On reflex, he turned his left wrist to look at his watch, and he screamed loud enough for the sound to echo through the building. He gasped for breath and groaned as he managed to get a glimpse of his watch face without turning his wrist any farther.

It was only 2:08 a.m. He had to get through four more hours before Barry and Duane would arrive.

How was he going to last that long?

He looked at his wrist again . . . and immediately wished he hadn't. He could see two broken bones poking against the underside of his skin. The sight made his stomach heave. He swallowed hard and took shallow breaths to keep himself from throwing up.

Hudson shifted carefully. His urine-stained underwear and jeans were irritating his skin. His butt and thighs were burning and itchy. He wanted to get out of the clothes. But how would he do that without jostling his wrist?

Maybe he could just stay where he was for the next four hours. Yeah, it would suck to sit on the hard floor with pee-saturated pants and a broken wrist. But wouldn't trying to move be worse?

Hudson nodded to himself and wiped his eyes with his right hand. His heart rate began to slow down.

Making that decision had calmed him somewhat. It had taken the pressure off.

Things weren't that bad, he told himself. Yes, his wrist was badly broken, and he'd have to go through all that pain again when he got it set, but at least it was his left hand. And a little pee in the pants never killed anyone. He was going to be okay.

"You're nothing," a voice said.

Hudson sucked in his breath and looked around.

"Less than nothing," the voice said.

Hudson reacted without thinking. He dropped the rolling pin and started to put both hands down so he could prepare to stand.

Again, his scream did a tour of the building. Fresh tears ran down his cheeks.

"Stop it!" he shouted.

He wasn't sure if he was yelling at himself about forgetting he had a broken wrist or if he was yelling at the voice.

High-pitched and nasally, Lewis's voice was unmistakable. So was the way he said "Nothing." He never made the *th* sound. His version of *nothing* sounded like "nutting."

"You're nothing but smoke," the Lewis voice said.

Hudson grabbed the rolling pin again and waved it in front of him uselessly. Then he tucked the rolling pin under his arm and bent over to cover his right ear with his right hand. Thankfully, he remembered not to use his left hand. But that meant that when the voice spoke again, saying, "You're nothing at all," Hudson could hear it just fine through his uncovered left ear.

"Go away!" Hudson begged the voice.

He knew it wasn't going to go away. So he wasn't surprised when he heard the Lewis voice say again, "Nothing. Nothing at all."

He *was* surprised, though, when he turned toward the sound and saw the decayed rabbit animatronic shuffling down the hall toward him. Staring intently at Hudson, the thing's mouth was moving. "Nothing," it said. "Less than nothing. Nothing but smoke."

And again. "Nothing. Less than nothing. Nothing but smoke." It was still Lewis's voice, but it was coming through the dreadful broken teeth of the rotting animatronic.

Hudson tried to shift in preparation for standing without moving his wrist. It didn't work. He had to move his left arm to get his right arm in position to push himself to an upright position.

The pain brought with it a wave of nausea. Hudson bent over, but the sound of the animatronic taking another clicking step forced him to move again.

Nearly hyperventilating, Hudson stood, his back to the wall.

Behind him, hands and arms brushed against his shoulder blades. He quickly stepped away from the wall, and he almost lost his balance. His legs felt weak. He was swaying like a sapling in the wind.

He looked at the rolling pin lying on the ground. He couldn't bend over to get it.

Move, he told himself. *You've got to move.*

He made himself look at the advancing animatronic. And that's when he saw the knife.

The knife got him to move. The animatronic was only a couple feet from the knife. Hudson had to get to it first.

Lunging forward, ignoring the pain in his wrist, Hudson was able to snatch up the knife just before the animatronic reached it. He took a step back and brandished the knife ahead of him.

The animatronic kept advancing. Hudson took another step back and waved the knife through the air.

The animatronic's pace didn't falter.

Hudson swung the knife wildly, back and forth and back and forth. The animatronic was on him, reaching for him, clawing at him . . . and suddenly the knife blade sliced through Hudson's bicep.

Hudson screamed, turned, and ran as scorching pain erupted in his arm. Warmth trickled down his bicep, through the crook of his elbow, and from his forearm to his injured wrist.

"Nothing divided in half is nothing," Lewis's voice called out behind Hudson.

Hudson nearly tripped and fell.

How could he have forgotten?

Lewis, the real Lewis, had said that very thing to him when Lewis had slashed Hudson with a knife just before the fire. The knife was the reason the fire happened. Why had Hudson suppressed that memory?

It didn't matter now. Nothing mattered except getting away from the robot corpse thing that was after him. He forced himself to move down the hall, but his steps faltered, and he had to grab the wall for support. One of the animatronic mouths bit his right forearm and he screamed, once again moving away from the wall.

He had to get out of this hallway. He started running, stumbling, staggering, weaving, but trying to stay in the center of the hall. Every jarring step was pain filled, but he kept going.

Reaching the far corner of the hallway, Hudson looked over his shoulder to see how close his pursuer was. He slid to a stop.

No one was behind him. The hallway was empty, and its walls were still.

Well, it wasn't completely empty. A bloody butcher knife lay on the floor near where Hudson was when the animatronic slashed him.

Or did it? Had he imagined it?

He looked down at his arm. He sure hadn't imagined that. A sickeningly wide gap in his skin ran from his upper bicep to just above his elbow. Blood was still gushing copiously down his arm, over his busted wrist, and dripping off his fingers.

He had to stop the bleeding. He started to put his right hand over the wound, but he paused. Why was his right hand bloody? He hadn't touched the wound yet.

It was bloody like it had been splashed with blood when it slashed—

No. He did not just slash himself. Did he?

Hudson shook his head several times and concentrated on how he was going to stop the bleeding in his arm.

He'd used up all his first aid supplies on his head wound.

Wavering on his feet, turning to look around him every two seconds, crying and unable to stop, Hudson tried to think. What should he do?

As he watched the flow of the blood, he realized it wouldn't flow as fast if his arm wasn't hanging down. So he lifted his arm. But he'd forgotten about his wrist . . . again.

The broken bones under the skin ground together as they rotated, and he screeched in pain. He tried to raise his arm above the level of his heart, but the pain wouldn't let him.

Panicking because he was starting to feel weak, Hudson

tore the wrap off his injured head and awkwardly tried to resituate it around his upper arm. There wasn't enough material to cover the entire wound.

Material.

Of course. He could use towels from the gift shop. And then he could break the front doors of the building and get out of here.

Hudson had to get to the lobby. Fast.

Once again surveying the hall to be sure he was alone and not under attack by the walls, Hudson walked as fast as he could toward the lobby. Every step jolted his wrist, and he had to fight the nausea that wanted him to sit down and stop moving.

"Keep going," he told himself. "Keep going. Don't stop again."

But nearly at the end of the hall, he did stop. He'd forgotten the rolling pin. He looked back down the hall.

The rolling pin was gone. And where were his nightstick and the hammer? The last he'd seen them was in the hands reaching from the walls.

Moaning, Hudson stared at the spot on the floor where he was sure he'd left the wooden utensil. He willed it to be there. But it wasn't.

Hudson whimpered and turned his back on what he couldn't explain.

He staggered forward again. Concentrating, he willed his feet to keep moving.

As he passed Pirate's Cove, Hudson told himself he was halfway there. "Just keep going," he ordered himself.

But then he stopped. He stopped in horror when the purple curtain around Pirate's Cove began ripping in half, torn from the inside by Foxy's pirate hook. Hudson gaped at what he was seeing. Was this happening, or had this exhibit's animation been completed without his knowledge?

As Hudson began shuffling away from Pirate's Cove, the curtain was wrenched apart, and the deformed rabbit animatronic peered out at Hudson. It raised its arm, and Hudson could see the rabbit held a Foxy arm. It was the rabbit that had been slashing the curtain.

Hudson ran.

Several feet down the hall, he checked over his shoulder. He wasn't being chased. But he didn't slow down. He had to get to the towels to stop his bleeding.

At least there was one good thing about the animatronic being behind him. It wouldn't be hanging in the inner hall, which Hudson realized he'd have to pass through to get to the lobby.

Squaring his shoulders, he forged ahead, turning down the hall where the animatronic was hanging at the start of the—

The animatronic was hanging on the wall, just where Barry and Duane left it.

How did it get back here?

Watching the horrible robotic character, Hudson shuffled past as fast as he could. The animatronic didn't move.

Hudson checked it several times after he passed it, but it kept hanging there. Silent. Still.

Finally, he concentrated on getting to his destination. He was almost there.

But every step he took, he felt weaker. He couldn't walk in a straight line. And his sight was getting a little blurry.

Determined, he worked his way down the long hall and made the turn toward the lobby. It took longer to get there than it should have. But he got there.

Unfortunately, the shop was mostly dark. Lights from the lobby barely reached the space; they provided only enough illumination to create amorphous shapes.

Stumbling into the darkened space, Hudson used his right hand to feel along the shelves. He groped for the textiles he knew were here.

Feeling fur, he made his way past the plushies and action figures.

Hey. Did something nip at him?

No, he was imagining things. Which was understandable, given what he'd experienced this evening.

He kept going, and he finally found the towels. He grabbed a stack of them and started wrapping them around his arm. When they wouldn't stay, he felt around until he found the Chica headbands he remembered were here. He used those to tie the towels in place.

It was an awkward and painful process. He had to keep moving his arm to position the towels and the bands, and every time he did, his wrist protested in blazing blasts of pain. He gritted his teeth, hissed out his breath, and kept working on wrapping his arm.

Finally, he finished. Now for the front door.

Still weak but encouraged by the progress he'd made, Hudson thought about what was in the gift shop. What could he use to break the glass door?

Sporting goods. Hadn't he seen a baseball bat in here?

Hudson took a step toward where he thought he'd find a bat, but a loud fluttering sound stopped him. He squinted into the darkness. He saw movement.

What was that?

He couldn't tell, but he could tell the movement was advancing his way. He backed out of the gift shop.

He was nearly out of the gift shop when he smelled something that made him throw up all over the floor. He couldn't help it. It was a reflex.

He smelled black cherry pipe tobacco.

And now he smelled the acidic stench of vomit.

"You going to mess your room, boy?" Lewis bellowed. "You can just stay there and breathe it in."

Hudson wavered on his feet, staring in amazement while Lewis stormed around his room and gathered every toy Hudson had ever owned. Piling them, lining them up, Lewis created a barrier at the doorway of Hudson's room.

"Live in the stink, little boy," Lewis growled.

Trying not to breathe through his nose, Hudson turned to his bed.

But his bed wasn't there. He wasn't in his room.

He was outside the gift shop.

Breathing through his nose, he took a step into the lobby. He had to get to the front doors.

But what happened next wasn't the way he'd planned to do it.

Hudson was suddenly lifted off the floor and up into the air. Then he was thrown across the lobby.

Somehow, as he flew through the air, Hudson was flipped over. He hit the wall on the opposite side of the lobby with his back, and a disturbing *crunch*, and more pain than his mind was able to fathom. He slid to the floor, landing on his left side . . . on his slashed arm and broken wrist. The initial impact felt just like it had when Lewis had thrown him into a wall, but the aftermath was worse.

When did Lewis do that? Was it before or after the barrier of toys?

Hudson couldn't remember.

Where was he now? Was he in his past or was he in the present?

He didn't know. All he knew was pain.

Hudson bellowed at the top of his lungs. Then he panted like a dog.

Was this the same injury? A new one? If it was new, had the fused disks held?

Hudson couldn't tell. His back was a radiating pulsation of pain. He lay still, afraid to ask anything else of his battered body.

As he lay on his side, breathing shallowly, he tried to check his surroundings. Was Lewis still in his room? Was the rabbit animatronic going to show up again?

He craned his neck to look all over the lobby. He saw nothing out of place.

No. Wait. Something *was* out of place.

On the wall above him, a large vent cover was hanging by one screw. The cover was swinging slowly, the dark passage it had concealed now wide open to anyone or anything.

Could the animatronic have thrown him and then retreated into the vent?

The sickly scent of cherry pipe tobacco hung in the air again.

He had to get away from the horror in this building.

Gingerly moving his legs, which made his back kink up in stiff protest, Hudson tried to get in a position so he could stand. No matter how much it hurt, he couldn't just lie here and let the animatronic, or whatever was tormenting him, make its next move.

He needed to get to the doors.

Hudson turned to look toward them. He gasped.

No way.

No . . . freaking . . . way.

He blinked, rubbed his eyes with his right hand and looked again.

Yes, he was seeing what he was seeing. The doors were being guarded by the gift shop's entire supply of plushies and action figures. They were lined up and poised for action. And they were all watching him.

Hudson stood . . . and screamed.

His back felt like it was being torn in half. His wrist felt like it was filled with ground glass. His arm was pounding out a staccato beat of intense, tortuous pain.

He couldn't take much more. He had to hide.

But where?

He looked up and down the halls stretching away from the lobby, and his gaze landed on the kitchen doorway at the far end of the left hall. Holding his breath, he took a step in that direction. He knew where he could go.

Heat purges, he could hear Granny's voice in his head. *Fire heals.*

The fireplace. He'd be safe in the fireplace. Lewis couldn't reach him there.

Heat purges. Fire heals.

Using these two phrases as a mantra, Hudson began shuffling toward the kitchen. Each step was a new elevation of the pain. Each of his footfalls made him wonder if he'd make it. When he asked himself if he'd make it, he told himself, "Heat purges. Fire heals."

He didn't mean the words literally. He had no intention of heating anything or setting fire to anything. But the words had reminded him of where he could hide. The words seemed to control his feet so they kept moving toward Hudson's destination.

When he reached it, he stood in front of it and smiled. He wondered why he hadn't thought of this before.

Hudson reached out with his right hand and tugged on one of the industrial oven doors. As soon as it opened, he gingerly climbed inside the oven. There he sat, stretched out his legs, and grabbed the door. He pulled it closed with a satisfying *whump*.

Finally, he was safe.

Or was he? As he huddled against the hard, cool walls

of the oven, Hudson's mind went back, once again, to the past.

Safe was what he thought he was the night he wrestled the knife from Lewis and threatened the man with it.

"Leave me alone!" he'd screamed. "Never touch me again, or I'll tell everyone everything."

Lewis had laughed at him. "Kid, you're not going to tell anyone anything. They'll think they know what they need to know."

And with that strange statement, Lewis had disappeared into the kitchen and Hudson had crawled into the fireplace to hide. The next thing Hudson knew, there was a fire in the fireplace . . . and then the house was on fire. Hudson barely got out alive. The burns on his legs left him with the nerve damage that had barred him from the Navy.

He didn't set the fire. Did he? He told everyone he didn't set it because he believed he didn't.

A popping sound yanked Hudson from his reverie.

What was that?

He listened.

And he heard a rustling sound and a snap.

Hudson hunched over in the fireplace, and he listened for Lewis as he looked at Lewis's lighter. When had Hudson taken it? He didn't remember, but it was his now.

Hudson could feel Lewis's lighter in his hand. He could feel his thumb on the little starter wheel. Flames started crawling up the curtains next to the fireplace.

In the oven, something whirred, then made a little

spitting sound. Hudson heard a concussive burst like a backdraft blowing open a door.

He looked down . . . at his empty hands.

The cool walls of the oven started warming up.

Hudson shot away from the oven walls.

No!

Panicked, Hudson kicked at the oven door. It didn't budge.

"Open the door!" he shouted.

He kicked again. The door remained closed.

"Oh, Hudson," a voice said.

It was Granny Foster!

Hudson looked around the oven and tried to see out through the thick glass opening in the door. He couldn't see anyone.

"Granny, get me out of here!" Hudson yelled.

"Oh, Hudson," Granny's voice repeated. Her voice wasn't coming from outside the oven. It was inside, with Hudson.

The oven got hotter.

Hudson started to sweat. "Help me!"

Hudson heard what sounded like a sigh rushing through the oven. "Your path is your path," Granny's voice said.

And the oven got hotter . . . and hotter.

"You know what I'm going to miss most when we start training?" Duane asked Barry as the two men climbed the steps to the front of Fazbear's Frights.

"What?" Barry pulled out his keys and unlocked the front doors. He was a little surprised he had to do that. Usually, Hudson was down here already unlocking the doors.

"Your grandma's cooking," Duane said.

Barry laughed, then sobered. "I would have said that, too, until I met Faith."

"That'll work out," Duane said as they stepped into the building.

"Where's Hudson?" Barry asked.

"Hudson!" Duane called.

"What's that smell?" Barry wrinkled up his face.

Duane covered his nose. "Smells like something burning. Hey, did you hear about the fire at the circus?"

"What?"

"It was in tents." Duane laughed loudly. "Get it? *In. Tents.*"

Barry shook his head. "Hudson!" he called.

They waited, breathing shallowly. No one answered.

"Let's go check the office," Barry said.

The men headed down the main hall. They looked around as they went. Everything was the same as it had been when they'd left the night before. Same stacks of boxes. Same animatronic they'd hooked to the wall.

Duane bent over. "I forgot to pick up this tooth last night. We can glue it back in."

They went down the hall and leaned into the open door of the office. It looked normal, too. But Hudson wasn't in it.

"Where the heck is he?" Duane asked.

Barry shook his head.

Duane laughed. "Maybe he finally got smart and left this crummy town."

"That wouldn't be a bad thing," Barry said. "I'd miss him, but he could use a fresh start."

Duane made a face. "The smell is stronger down here."

"It's coming from the kitchen, I think," Barry said.

"Let's go check it out."

As the two headed toward the kitchen, Barry said, "I feel for Hudson. Poor guy deserves to have something go right."

ABOUT THE AUTHORS

Scott Cawthon is the author of the bestselling video game series *Five Nights at Freddy's*, and while he is a game designer by trade, he is first and foremost a storyteller at heart. He is a graduate of The Art Institute of Houston and lives in Texas with his family.

Andrea Rains Waggener is an author, novelist, ghostwriter, essayist, short story writer, screenwriter, copywriter, editor, poet, and a proud member of Kevin Anderson & Associates' team of writers. In a past she prefers not to remember much, she was a claims adjuster, JCPenney's catalog order-taker (before computers!), appellate court clerk, legal writing instructor, and lawyer. Writing in genres that vary from her chick-lit novel, *Alternate Beauty*, to her dog how-to book, *Dog Parenting*, to her self-help book, *Healthy, Wealthy, & Wise*, to ghostwritten memoirs to ghostwritten YA, horror, mystery, and mainstream fiction projects, Andrea still manages to find time to watch the rain and obsess over her dog and her knitting, art, and music projects. She lives with her husband and said dog on the Washington Coast, and if she isn't at home creating something, she can be found walking on the beach.

The first thing Larson was aware of when he fought through the cloudy filaments of unconsciousness was the beeping. The next thing he noticed was the smell—an off-putting combination of chicken soup, urine, and bleach. Finally, the rest of his senses kicked in. His eyes squeezed shut against an assault of bright light, and his body squirmed in reaction to pain in his gut, his ribs, his head, his side, and the back of his hand. He also wasn't happy with the dry, cottony feel of his mouth. He worked his tongue around his teeth as he hesitantly opened his eyes.

"There you are!" a chirpy female voice said. Larson grimaced but turned toward the sound.

A rosy-faced petite woman in a pink nurse's uniform hovered over him. The nurse was cute—dark-haired and green-eyed. Her nametag read ANITA STARLING. Larson felt her warm fingers against his skin as she touched the back of his hand, near the area that hurt.

He groaned as he tried to shift so he could see what was wrong with his hand.

"Uh-uh," Anita said. "Your stomach muscles aren't ready for that kind of thing yet."

The source of the hand pain was an IV needle poking beneath his skin. Larson frowned at it. He tried to form a question, but his mouth was too dry.

Anita moved away and picked up a small paper cup holding a bendable straw. "Here." She lifted the cup near his chin and tucked the straw between his lips. He sucked in water, blessedly wet and cool.

"Not too much," she warned. "You had a nasty infection, and you underwent a rather long surgery. Your body isn't ready to guzzle water."

"Infection?" Larson managed. His voice sounded like it had been shredded by a cheese grater. He cleared his throat as he tried to piece together the last thing he could remember.

"I'll get the doctor in here to explain it to you," Anita said. "All I know is that it was a bizarre infection, and it was apparently killed by whatever burned your stomach."

"Burned?" Larson asked. He idly wondered how long he'd be speaking in single-word questions.

Anita adjusted the scratchy blanket that was tucked under Larson's chin. "Like I said, I'll get the doctor in here. He can probably tell you more."

★ ★ ★

As it turned out, the doctor wasn't much help. When he visited Larson later that day, he told Larson the infection couldn't be identified.

The detective had a hand-sized third-degree burn on his belly. The doctor asked Larson if he knew what had caused it. Larson feigned ignorance. By the time the doctor had come in, Larson had recovered a hazy memory of the Stitchwraith kneeling next to him, putting a red-hot hand against Larson's stomach. But he wasn't about to try to describe that to the doctor.

Once Larson was home and recovering in his apartment, he began champing at the bit to get back to work. The chief had other ideas, though; Larson was on leave until he received medical clearance.

At least the convalescence gave Larson more time to spend with Ryan. His ex-wife was letting the boy visit every day, and the video and board games Larson and Ryan played helped pass the time.

Even so, Larson had endless hours at night to think about the events at the factory. And he'd come to a tentative conclusion.

The conclusion was strange and surprising . . . so surprising that Larson was having trouble accepting it. Even so, he was pretty sure his reasoning was sound.

He strongly suspected that the Stitchwraith wasn't evil after all.

After Larson was free of whatever they'd given him for pain at the hospital, his memory of the inexplicable events at the factory became perfectly clear. He could see every detail in his mind's eye, and two of them were standing out: 1) the Stitchwraith had appeared to resist being drawn into Afton's Amalgamation, and 2) the Stitchwraith had burned the infection out of Larson's belly.

These two details, unless Larson was misinterpreting them, seemed to suggest pretty clearly that the Stitchwraith wasn't as bad as Larson had thought it was. If the Stitchwraith was Afton, as Larson had thought, why would it have held itself apart from the trash monster? And if it was Afton, why had it removed the infection?

Larson intended to find the Stitchwraith. He needed to determine exactly what the thing was, whether it was evil or not.

That, however, would have to wait. Larson had a more pressing problem to deal with first.

It was 2:25 a.m., and Larson was lying in his bed staring at the spidering patterns of light the streetlamps threw across his ceiling fan. For at least the tenth time since he came home from the hospital, he was trying to figure out what was happening to him. Because something was wrong, very wrong.

Larson's physical wounds were healing well. Each day, the pain from his injuries lessened a bit. But he was experiencing a mental symptom that quite frankly terrified him . . . so much so that Larson had asked his doctor for a CAT scan to be sure he hadn't suffered a brain injury. When the doctor asked why this was needed, Larson was vague. "Weird vision issues," he'd said.

The CAT scan didn't uncover anything wrong with Larson's brain. That was both good . . . and potentially bad.

The web-like chiaroscuro that held Larson's attention was blurry, and Larson was trying to bring it into focus. As always when he had one of the episodes he was having right then, he felt dizzy and everything around him devolved into a nearly transparent haze.

Through that haze, Larson was seeing things he shouldn't have been able to see. He was getting glimpses into the past.

These glimpses weren't like daydreams, like the mental pictures that he could summon up when he let his mind wander. These glimpses were real . . . or at least they *seemed* real. They were memories, but not his own. These images belonged to others, from different places and different times.

Right now, for instance, beyond the shadows on his ceiling, Larson was watching Freddy Fazbear and the other animatronics that had been all the rage when Freddy Fazbear's Pizza was in its heyday as they performed a rousing rendition of an '80s rock song Larson hadn't heard in years. The music was so loud and its bass so intense that Larson could feel the beat vibrating his mattress.

That was the strange thing about these visions he was having. He wasn't just seeing things from the past. He was *experiencing* them. In addition to the vibrations that fluttered through his body, Larson could smell fresh pizza. Since all he'd eaten earlier was a frozen turkey dinner and some popcorn he'd shared with Ryan, he had no explanation for the aromas of tomato sauce and cheese that seemed to waft around him.

As Larson watched the animatronics perform on a stage that looked like it was filling his bedroom, the scene shifted. This was another thing that was freaky. Not only was he dropping into these lifelike vignettes, but they also changed constantly. One minute he was in Freddy Fazbear's pizza. The next, he was at the movie theater. The next minute, he was hanging out with his friends; or at least someone else's friends. But always, no matter how many times he jumped from one scene to the next, the filler—that's how he'd come to think of it—between the scenes was always the same. As his mind swept him from one visit to the past to another, he always saw the same thing in between: he saw a ball pit.

The weird thing about the ball pit was that Larson

couldn't remember ever having seen it in real life. Sure, he'd seen a ball pit before; Ryan had liked playing in them when he was really little. But Ryan hadn't played in *this* ball pit.

The ball pit that Larson kept seeing was a disgusting ball pit. It was old, and the balls' red, blue, and green plastic surfaces were faded. They were also woolly with dust and mildew, as if they hadn't been touched in decades. They smelled, too, not only of that dust and mildew but of something else, something coppery and decaying.

Also, it wasn't entirely accurate to say that Larson just *saw* the ball pit. He actually experienced it, as if he were in it. When the ball pit appeared to him, he could feel the grubby plastic around him, like he was swimming through beads of sphere-shaped water. Except it didn't feel clean like water. In addition to the dusty, mildewy film that made the balls feel scummy, the plastic seemed to have something viscous on it. The spheres tried to adhere to him like Velcro.

Larson blinked when his dizziness abruptly went away and his bedroom came back into focus. This always happened. The visions left him as quickly as they appeared each time.

Larson sat up and rubbed his eyes. He rose and shuffled into the kitchen for a drink of water.

Standing in front of his sink, he gazed out the small window above it. The night was stormy. All he could see was blackness and rain spotting the panes. He shivered as he ran water into a glass.

Gulping the water, he turned away from the window. "Enough," he said out loud.

It was time for Larson to get back to work. And the first thing he needed to do was find the ball pit. He was seeing it for a reason. It had to be related to all the other weirdness he'd experienced. He was going to figure out how it fit into the rest of the puzzle.

★ ★ ★

Pulling his cloak tighter around his doll face, Jake picked his way down a narrow alley. Rain was falling steadily, and even though Jake's doll-face eyes weren't real, it still felt weird to have water in them.

Jake was happy he'd found the cloak he was wearing. It wasn't waterproof—he thought it was made of wool— but it was heavy and it kept most of the water off his face and metal body. It also hid what he was, a little. He still had to keep to the dark back streets, the corners and crevices of the world.

Jake had been hiding for nine full sunrises and sunsets since he'd left the factory. During that time, he'd felt sadder than he could ever remember being. He missed having Andrew with him in this strange thing he was in. And he felt overwhelmed by the knowledge he carried—that something bad was out there.

He'd thought about trying to find the bad thing, but what could he do about it if he found it? Besides, he was scared.

As Jake passed an open dumpster pressed up against the outer wall of a tall brick building, he heard a scuttling sound. He watched a rat scurry down the side of the dumpster's scarred green metal. When the rat scampered toward the edge of the brick wall, Jake spotted an old, worn hiking boot . . . that moved when the rat ran past it.

Jake stopped and peered behind the dumpster.

The boot was attached to a man who had long hair and a tangled beard. Jake couldn't tell the man's age. He also couldn't tell whether the man was alive. The man's foot had twitched, but his face was pale and his eyes were closed.

Suddenly, the squawk of a siren and the flash of bright headlights invaded the alley. Jake didn't hesitate. He dropped into a squat next to the man.

Water sluiced over Jake. It was overflowing the building's gutters, dropping to the ground in almost-solid, wet sheets.

The siren screeched again, and a shout rang out. Jake shrank back against the wall.

As Jake moved, he lost his balance, and he put out a hand to steady himself. His hand landed on the man's shoulder. When it did, the man groaned and moved, exhaling a rank, garlicky breath.

Oh no! Jake thought.

He immediately felt a wave of suffocating regret. He'd killed another person!

But wait. The man didn't stop breathing. Jake could hear the man's snorting exhales. No black blood ran down his face. He was alive!

The siren sounds stopped, but Jake could still see the glow of the headlights. Above the patter of the rain, he could hear raised voices.

Despite what he could see and hear, though, Jake's consciousness was no longer in the alley. He found himself in a cozy, bright dining room.

The dining room was dominated by an old oak table around which sat a happy family. At first, the mom and dad and two children laughing and eating didn't seem at all familiar to Jake. However, as he watched them share pot roast and stories about their days, he realized he was seeing a slightly younger, happier version of the man lying behind the dumpster.

Jake didn't know why he was getting a glimpse into the man's past, but he liked it. The scene was so heartwarming; all of the sadness that had weighed on him over the past few days began to disappear . . . until the scene abruptly changed.

Suddenly, the dining room was gone, and Jake was yanked harshly through what he figured were the man's memories. At eye-boggling superspeed, Jake watched the man go to work, come home, play with his kids, have dates with his wife, and go on trips with his whole family. It was like riding a fast train through an amusement park.

But then the happy train crashed. It was a real crash—real for the man, anyway. Jake's good feelings collapsed into grief as he watched the man crawl from the wreckage of his family van. He wailed in despair as emergency workers pulled his dead family one by one from the crumpled metal.

Devasted by what he was seeing, Jake started to remove his metal hand from the man. Jake didn't want to feel what this man felt then, the sharp loss the man still felt now. But Jake also couldn't stand to leave the man caught in this web of misery. What if Jake could do something to help?

Jake concentrated, and he sent his thoughts back through the soup of memories he'd just seen. Maybe he could pull one out, a good one, and make it bigger and brighter than the rest. If he could, he could ease the man's pain.

He had to try.

Jake knew exactly which memory to make the biggest. It was the first one—the happy family dinner.

Jake put all his focus on that memory. He pushed his intention into it so it puffed up in his mind; it was almost like blowing up a balloon—only the balloon was a memory and the air was Jake's will. Jake made the memory bigger and bigger, and then he gently suggested it back to the man's unconscious mind. In a way, he put the man's mind inside the bubble of that one happy scene.

And then Jake let go of the man. As soon as he did, he was back in the alley.

The rain was coming down harder now, and the voices Jake had heard before were coming closer. Jake had to get out of there.

First, though, he looked down at the man to make sure he was okay. And Jake was happy to see that the man's face was no longer contorted with pain. In fact, the man looked like he might have been smiling. And his breathing was softer, more even.

A clatter and the sound of footsteps spurred Jake to action. He leaned forward and looked around the corner of the dumpster.

Two men were making their way down the alley toward where Jake hid. They'd find him if he didn't do something!

Jake looked around. There was no way he'd be able to run off without being seen. But behind him, a small door led into the brick building whose gutter was spilling water over the dumpster. Jake quickly grasped the door-knob and wrenched it. The door gave way, and he slipped into the darkness inside.

Closing the door behind him, Jake stood next to it for several seconds, listening. The rain could still be heard in there, but otherwise, the place was silent. Pressing his hands against the door to keep it closed, he waited to see if the men would try to open it.

After several minutes, he relaxed. They must have moved on.

Jake turned and surveyed his surroundings. A weak glow from a sputtering streetlight came through a dirty window a few feet from the door. It was enough to reveal stacks of boxes and crates. He was in some kind of storage room.

Jake moved farther into the room and lowered his endoskeleton onto a crate. He threw back the hood of his cloak and thought about what had just happened. What he'd been able to do was pretty cool. But how did he do it? He didn't know, but just thinking about how he'd been able to help that man—even if just for that night—made him a little less sad. Maybe he could do more than just lurk in the dark. Maybe he could do something good.

As soon as Jake had this thought, he heard a muffled scrape. Standing, he looked around again. He still saw only boxes and crates, but when he heard a faint snore, he started looking behind the stacks.

Just past the third stack he explored, Jake found a tall, skinny teenage girl.

Wearing just a thin, gray T-shirt and ripped jeans, the girl was curled on her side, asleep. She looked cold, so Jake took off his cloak and bent down to cover her.

When he crouched next to her, he realized that she was more passed out than asleep. Her face was slack, and the circles under her eyes were so dark they looked like smudges of charcoal.

Jake tucked his cloak around the girl, and as he did, a scene from an old TV commercial flashed through his mind. It was one of the anti-drug commercials that stamped the slogan "Just say no" across scenes of pale, passed-out skinny teens. This girl looked like one of the ones in the commercial.

Jake frowned as he gazed at the girl. He knew how destructive drugs could be; drugs killed people! This poor girl was in trouble. She obviously needed help. Maybe Jake could do something for her.

Studying the girl in the muted light, he saw that if she hadn't been so pale and thin, she might have been pretty. She had long, reddish-brown hair that was thick and wavy. It was dirty and tangled now, but he thought it could look nice if it were washed and brushed. He couldn't see the girl's eyes, but her features were nice. As he looked at her face, though, he noticed that her lips were dry and cracked.

She needed water.

Looking around once again, Jake managed to find a discarded plastic container. He took the container to the door, opened the door a couple inches to check outside, and, when he didn't see anyone, he stepped out and held the container under the heavy rain. It only took a few seconds to fill the container, and once that was done, Jake ducked back inside the room. He hurried over to see if he could get the girl to swallow the water.

The girl moaned when Jake nudged her lips with the container. He frowned, not sure what to do next.

Before he could figure it out, the door behind him swung open, the wind blowing rain into the room. It blew in something else, too.

Two men swept through the open door. One of them slammed it closed.

Although Jake wasn't at all hidden from the men, the room was so dim that he was pretty sure they didn't see what he was at first. Or if they did, they didn't seem to care.

"What are you doing in here?" one of the men growled.

This man was the smaller of the two, but that wasn't saying much. Both men were tall and broad-shouldered.

Jake could tell that neither man was a nice man. One of them was scowling, and the other had features that were settled into what was probably a permanent sneer. They both had dark, mean eyes.

"Are you deaf?" the second man asked. "He asked you a question."

The second man, whose face was covered with old scars, stomped over and kicked at Jake. Jake didn't react, but the movement and the sound woke up the girl. She opened her eyes—they were a deep blue—and immediately, she hugged herself, curling up tighter as if she could wrap her body in a cocoon of safety. She was clearly afraid of the scar-faced man.

When the girl's gaze flitted to the second man and she tried to scoot backward, Jake could see that she knew both of them. Jake shifted his attention back to the men.

Jake was pretty sure they were dealers.

The two men started approaching. Jake decided he needed to make them go away. He stood up.

Now that Jake was upright, the men couldn't fail to see Jake's metal endoskeleton. It didn't seem to faze them, though. Both men gave Jake a nonchalant once-over.

"What are you supposed to be?" the scar-faced man asked.

The other man laughed. "Get lost on your way to a costume party?"

When Jake didn't respond, Scar-face charged toward him. "Get out of the way, punk!" He pointed at the girl. "She owes me money!"

Jake didn't move. He wasn't going to let these men bully the poor girl. He crossed his arms because he thought it would make him look tougher.

The men sidestepped Jake as if he were nothing. As Jake turned, Scar-face strode to the girl and kicked her leg. "Where's my money, you piece of trash?"

"Hey!" Jake shouted. "Leave her alone!"

Both men laughed, and Scar-face pulled out a knife. Before he could do anything with it, though, Jake took a quick step forward. He didn't think. He just acted. His anger and outrage were driving him.

Jake grabbed the scowling man and lifted him easily. Dangling the man in front of him, Jake shook him hard.

The man immediately went from sarcastic jerk to sniveling kid. He started crying.

"Please, please," the big man begged. "I didn't mean . . ."

Jake didn't bother to listen to whatever the man was going to say. He was too angry to hear clearly anyway. It felt like an ocean was roaring in his head. He could feel heat pulsing through his endoskeleton.

Jake gave the man another violent shake; then he tossed him through the window. Glass shattered and sprayed. Rain spattered in through the hole the man's body had made.

Jake turned toward the other man.

The man with the scar held up his hands and cowered away from Jake. "Hey, it's just business!" He was whining like a kid, too.

Jake didn't care. He stepped forward and backhanded the man across the jaw. The man went flying into a stack of boxes. He rolled onto the ground, and Jake dropped down on top of him.

Jake's rage burned even hotter, and when he pointed a finger at the man's face, his finger was glowing red hot. Jake studied the man's cruel eyes.

Easily holding the struggling man down, Jake thought for a few seconds. He bent over and held the tip of his metal finger against the man's forehead.

A few minutes later, Jake stepped out of the alleyway and looked up and down the main street. The girl, cradled in his arms, had passed out again. She felt nearly weightless to Jake.

Jake shifted his cloak so it covered her face. Then he

strode down the street, searching for a safe place where he could take care of her.

★ ★ ★

After two days of rain, the sun had come out, and everything—still damp from the storm—seemed to glitter in the brightness. Or maybe that was just Larson's mood. He was feeling good.

Well, maybe not *good*. But better.

He spent most of the morning tracking down buildings that might contain the ball pit that kept sucking him away from the real world. The threads he pulled at were serpentine, and they resulted in a list of a dozen possible locations.

Over the next couple hours, Larson visited more decrepit, boarded-up arcades than he'd cared to see, but eventually, his search led him to the derelict place he stood in front of now.

A tired-looking man gave Larson the key to what appeared to be an old restaurant. Then the old guy shuffled off as if he didn't care at all what Larson might do to the place.

Larson could see why. The cavernous dining room he stood in held nothing but cracked vinyl booths and scarred tables. The tables were lined up on a black-and-white checkerboard floor, and the booths hugged pale yellow walls that had vague shapes attempting to peek through the wall's bad paint job. In addition to the tables and booths, the room held an empty stage and a bare dance floor that looked forlorn under a smudged, broken mirror ball.

The room was thick with dust. Whole civilizations of

dust bunnies wafted when Larson moved.

The air in the place smelled musty. It was also vaguely sour, like the inside of a refrigerator filled with spoiled food. Larson put the back of his hand to his nose.

As soon as Larson had entered the place, he'd spotted what he was looking for. The ball pit was in the back-right corner of the room. Cordoned off by a dingy yellow rope, the ball pit warned away potential visitors with a sign that read, DO NOT USE.

"Who would try?" Larson muttered as he walked toward the place that had commandeered his consciousness so many times in the past few days.

It wasn't a figment of his imagination. It actually existed. And it clearly wanted him to find it . . . which was disturbing in the extreme.

Larson glanced over his shoulder and gave himself a mental shake. He was a cop, for Pete's sake. He wasn't scared of a stupid ball pit . . . was he?

Larson crossed over to the limp, dirty yellow rope. He lifted it, ducked beneath it, and stepped up to the edge of the ball pit. He studied the plastic balls.

They looked exactly the same as they did in his visions. They were dusty, mildewy, and faded.

He reached out and picked one up. It was just as he knew it would be: rough and somehow sticky, like it wanted to cling to his skin. He frowned and scraped a fingernail over the sphere's surface. Something flaky, almost charred-looking, coated the plastic.

Larson wanted to drop the filthy ball.

But Larson wasn't there to be grossed out. He was there to investigate. So, he didn't drop the ball. Instead, he held it up in front of his gaze and examined it closely. He frowned. The substance covering the plastic surface looked like blood. Old, old blood.

Larson took out his penknife and dug an evidence bag from his pocket. He took scrapings off the ball. Then he examined a few more plastic balls. All had the same substance on their surfaces. Larson took multiple samples.

When he was done, he stepped back and stared at the creepy pit. Finally, he shook off the heebie-jeebies that gripped him and left the abandoned restaurant.

★　★　★

The young doctor was wiped out, which was normal. She was on the tail end of a triple shift, and the stream of patients coming through the ER never ended.

Brushing hair from her face, the doctor pushed through the door to Exam Room 4/5. The room had two beds separated by a curtain. She shoved the curtain back and looked at the two patients in the side-by-side beds.

Both patients were men. Both looked like drug dealers. She'd seen their kind too many times to count.

The bigger man had come into the ER screaming, but after the doctor had determined he had a broken collarbone, she'd ordered a morphine drip. That man was now drifting in la-la land.

The second man wasn't as badly injured, but his forehead appeared to be burned.

The doctor pulled a treatment tray up to the man's side. She reached for some gauze.

"Let's get this cleaned up and see what needs to be done," she said.

He didn't respond. He just moaned.

The doctor blotted at the man's forehead for a few seconds. Then she stopped. She sucked in her breath.

Now that she'd cleaned up the area, she could see that someone had burned the words JUST SAY NO into the man's forehead!

*　*　*

Near the railroad tracks along the edge of town, a small maintenance shed squatted well away from anything else in the area. It was padlocked when Jake found it, but he'd easily removed the lock.

Now Jake and the girl were safely tucked inside the small building. The girl was still asleep. Jake was watching her carefully.

Jake found the shed right before dawn. After he put the girl inside, he went back out and quickly foraged for something to make her more comfortable. He found some blankets in a nearby dumpster, and he came back to layer the driest of them over her frail form.

Soon after night gobbled up dusk, the rain, which had left the area that morning, returned. A steady drumming now pounded on the tin roof above Jake's head. It sounded like a troupe of gnomes tap-dancing to music Jake couldn't hear.

The clamor didn't seem to bother the girl. She occasionally murmured in her sleep, and sometimes she kicked out as if fending off an unseen assailant. But mostly, she was quiet and still.

Jake sat next to her, watching over her. He also watched the door. Although he'd secured it with some rope he'd found in the shed, he was on alert. He didn't know who else might be after the girl, or when they might come looking for her.

For the first couple hours after nightfall, all was

quiet—except for the gnome dancing. However, when the rain let up enough for Jake to hear an owl hoot nearby, he heard something else . . . something that had him standing, poised to fight.

Outside the shed, something scraped across the wood siding. After the scrape, a metallic rattle cascaded down the door, then seemed to scrabble up the wall next to it. Then something thumped on the roof and clicked down the other side of the shed.

Jake traced the movement carefully. Something was out there. Something was *crawling* out there. He was sure of it.

Jake pulled his metal legs close to his body and edged nearer to the girl. He knew he was currently occupying a big endoskeleton, but right this second, he didn't feel like that. He felt like the kid he really was.

Something was outside the shed, scrabbling around it as if trying to find a way in. Jake cocked his head, listening. He put an arm protectively over the girl, just in case whatever was out there broke through the roof.

But he also trembled. He wished someone was there to put an arm over him, too.